D0626995

THE QUIET WOMAN

OTHER FIVE STAR TITLES BY TERENCE FAHERTY:

Dance in the Dark

The Quiet Woman

Terence Faherty

FIVE STAR
A part of Gale, Cengage Learning

GALE
CENGAGE Learning·

Farmington Hills, Mich • San Francisco • New York • Waterville, Maine
Meriden, Conn • Mason, Ohio • Chicago

GALE
CENGAGE Learning®

LIBRARY OF CONGRESS CATALOGING-IN-PUBLICATION DATA

Faherty, Terence.
    The quiet woman / Terence Faherty. — First edition.
      pages cm
    ISBN 978-1-4328-2868-4 (hardcover) — ISBN 1-4328-2868-1 (hardcover)
    1. Women novelists—Fiction. 2. Murder—Investigation—Fic-tion. I. Title.
  PS3556.A342Q84 2014
  813'.54—dc23   2014003150

First Edition. First Printing: June 2014
Find us on Facebook– https://www.facebook.com/FiveStarCengage
Visit our website– http://www.gale.cengage.com/fivestar/
Contact Five Star™ Publishing at FiveStar@cengage.com

Printed in the United States of America
1 2 3 4 5 6 7 18 17 16 15 14

For Kathryn and Dick Kennison

ACKNOWLEDGEMENTS

The Camelot Guide to Romance Writing, which is quoted forty-five times on the following pages, does not exist. Some of the tips I attribute to it are things I've figured out during my twenty-year career as a mystery writer and some are bits of advice I've picked up while listening to other writers talk about their craft. To add more romance-writing flavor, I consulted and can recommend three books that are more reliable than *The Camelot Guide* and have the further advantage of being real: *On Writing Romance,* by Leigh Michaels; *Writing Romances,* edited by Rita Gallagher and Rita Clay Estrada; and *Writing Exotic Romance,* by Alison Kent.

I would also like to thank Richard J. Sveum, MD (and BSI), for his suggestions on medical issues.

Prologue:
On the Screeb Road

Just after closing time they set out from Ryan's in the old Morris. Set out slowly because a fog had rolled in off Galway Bay sometime during the evening's drinking and bantering and darts, a fog like steam from a kettle, steam that came and went in white billows.

Two rode in the little car: Michael Murray, an automobile mechanic, and Agnes, his wife and the mother of his three children, all of whom had died within days of their birth.

So they were alone, these two, but not alone, as the three dead children were always with them, never far from Agnes's mind and therefore never far from Michael's. This was especially true tonight. Agnes had spent a long evening seated in the parlor bar, listening to other women talk of their children, a secret knife to her heart. The passage of years and years had eased the pain to this extent: Her friends' children had grown up and so their resemblance to the dead babies had dwindled away. But now an unlooked-for blow had struck. The oldest of these grown children had begun to have children of their own. And so the baby snaps had appeared again and with them the old regret.

"Don't drive into the ditch, Michael," Agnes said with a warning tap of her wedding band on the metal dashboard.

"Thank God you spoke," her husband replied. "For I was that close to doing it. I thought the fog might be less down there, due to the added air pressure."

"You're adding to the air pressure in here," she said, "blathering away like that. Roll your window down if you feel it come on you again and you'll clear the road for half a mile before us."

Michael smiled in the darkness at this victory. He knew from long experience what she'd been thinking of and he also knew how to distract her, which was to draw her attention to some foible of his own. Even their oldest friends thought of them as a bickering couple, not recognizing their back-and-forth for what it was, the grasp of a loving hand and an answering squeeze.

"It's a well-known fact," Michael continued, "that the density of the air increases the lower down you go, just as the weight of the water increases the lower you go in the sea. I've often observed it in the shop when the stove isn't drawing right. The smoke will hang in the air just above my head like a blanket, supported invisibly from below."

His wife sniffed only, and he saw he had made a misstep by mentioning his shop, which was in the nave of an abandoned church. Agnes sometimes superstitiously attributed their sad losses to his having desecrated that sacred place with his grease and oil.

He hurried on. "Sure I've noticed the same phenomenon in St. Timothy's with the incense."

"With the incense in St. Tim's," she repeated sarcastically. "I'd say instead it was the pipe smoke in Ryan's, if I thought you were up to observing anything in there except the new girl behind the sticks, that Sybil of the half-buttoned blouses. I could tell you what's holding her up, and it's not the density of the air."

Now they were set for the entire ride, having hit on a subject that would easily last them its last miles. That is, they would have been set but for a particularly dense patch of fog blowing across the road just then. Michael missed a turn he never missed, and a gray stone wall shot up before them like a cold hand thrust up from the turf.

"Michael!" Agnes screamed, but he was already standing on the brakes, pushing himself away from the wheel with one arm while throwing the other across her as they slid on the grassy verge. Their front bumper actually tapped the wall, but only that, and they were stopped, so close to the stones that they trapped the light from the old headlamps.

"Mary Mother of God," Agnes said and made the Sign of the Cross.

"I've scratched the chrome, I think," Michael said.

"Chrome," Agnes repeated as he backed them onto the road. "There's less chrome left on this car than hairs on your head, Michael Murray. Go slowly now. Haven't you learned your lesson?"

"I am going slowly," her husband replied, but in truth he was going faster and faster, her remark about his thinning hair having hit near the bone and dampened his earlier solicitude. Then too, he was embarrassed at having missed the turn and anxious to prove himself the master of the road.

"Slow down, Michael, won't you? You'll be off the road again."

"I'll not be. Not again."

"Then you'll hit something in the road."

"That's the beauty of a night like this. No thinking thing will be—"

Before he could finish, they saw the shape out in the very tips of their headlight beams. A little eddy in the fog? Yes. No! A figure, a woman, her back to them.

Michael stamped on the tiny brake pedal again, his left arm across his wife and her two wrapped around it. They were on pavement this time and not grass, and they stopped quickly but with a great noise of tires.

Quickly, but not before Agnes had taken in a mind's picture of the figure that would last her, unfading, all her life. It was of a woman of middling height and slender, wearing a brown cloth

11

coat with a bit of ornamental belt in the back, held in place by two bone buttons. Her head was covered by a bright blue scarf that shimmered like silk and completely hid her hair.

"What in God's name?" Michael asked, panting, for it was clear the woman wasn't walking in the road, only standing there. What was more, she had yet to acknowledge the Morris, hadn't so much as drawn herself in as it slid to a stop a few feet behind her.

Michael raised his palm above the horn, and at that moment the woman turned her head to them. They saw that it was barely a woman, a girl really, with a sweet wan face and eyes that were lost and imploring.

"What in God's name?" Michael said again and reached for his window crank. He'd no sooner grasped it than he turned to his wife. "Lower your window; she's coming to your side of the car."

"Are you blind then?" his wife said. "She's coming to your side of the car."

Their eyes met for a second in awe and fear. When they looked again to the fog, the girl was gone.

"Bridey," Agnes whispered.

"God save us. Do you think?"

Her nod was so slow and so deep it was almost a bow. "Bridey Finnerman." And she blessed herself again.

CHAPTER ONE

"Start on the darkest night of your heroine's life.
Then shoot out the lights."
—*Camelot Guide to Romance Writing*

What time was it in Ireland? Danny Furey looked at her watch, or tried to. The cabin of the 747 was too dark for her to see its hands but not dark enough to activate their cheap luminous paint. Was Ireland time five hours ahead of Jersey time? Four? Six? That was something she'd know if she'd had time to plan the trip like a rational human being. And she'd know the average temperature in Ireland in September and the average inches of rainfall. For that matter, she'd know the name of the hotel where she'd be sleeping that night.

Sleep. How many hours until they turned on the cabin lights and served breakfast? No more than two, and she was wasting them. *On your mark, get set, sleep,* Danny told herself, and almost smiled.

She looked to her right, to her brother Kerry. The Furey nose was just visible above the outline of the little airliner pillow, and Danny could tell from the sounds that nose was making that Kerry was deeply under. Kerry, who had violated every guidebook rule for avoiding the sleeplessness that led to jet lag, starting with not touching any alcohol. Kerry, who had a disease with a name so long he couldn't spell it, was sleeping away like he hadn't a care in the world.

13

As Danny turned from her brother, she felt the slight moistening of her palms she knew to be an early sign of airsickness. But she was rarely airsick, and only in very little planes in very bumpy skies. This plane was a great sky liner and the night air was very smooth, with just the occasional thump to make the overhead compartments rattle. It was like the motion of a train, she thought, right down to the slight swaying of the tail section where the Furey luck had landed them. Danny wasn't going to be sick—she was sure of that—but now that she'd let the possibility enter her mind, she couldn't put it out again.

She searched for some distracting thought and blundered, seizing on her most vivid recent memory: Kerry's phone call of the night before.

Just hearing from her brother on a day that wasn't her birthday or Jesus's had surprised Danny. The call had come in at twelve thirty-five by her bedside clock. Awakened from the first deep hour of sleep and slow-witted, Danny had decided that Kerry was drunk. Drunkenness was an even more likely explanation for a call than a birthday or Christmas, but it had turned out to be no more true.

"Pack your bags, little sister," Kerry said in place of hello. "We're going to find Letterfenny at long last."

Letterfenny. Asleep or awake, Danny spotted that warning word, that code for the unspecified future time when all would be right between herself and her brother and perhaps with North and South Korea as well.

"Someday," she said, but even that sounded too much like a contract. "Maybe."

"Not someday. Tomorrow. September 14, 2008. I've booked the seats. And not maybe. My last maybe is behind me. I'm all yeses and noes now. Noes mostly. I want Letterfenny to be a yes, and I need your help."

"Call me this weekend—"

"I'm sick, Danny. Chronic lymphocytic leukemia. That's the good kind, by the way. Kills you so slowly you might outlive it. Die of something else, I mean. At least, you might if you wait until you're sixty something to get it, like most people do. I got it at thirty-nine, which was spotting it way too much of a head start.

"I'll worry about that when we get back from Ireland, with Letterfenny struck off my to-do list. By the way, what you're feeling right now is the sensation of being backed into a corner."

Danny had felt the bile rise in her throat then and she felt it now. She thought of the little paper sack in the pocket of the seatback in front of her. But that seatback was now fully reclined, the balding head of its occupant almost in Danny's face, the pocket somewhere in the blackness beneath the head. Not that it mattered. She knew she'd strangle before she'd vomit into a bag in the dark, surrounded by strangers, asleep or pretending to be.

She wiggled out of her seat and into an aisle that was lit like a tiny runway, lights in the floor at intervals to outline the narrow path. She made her way to the back of the plane at a wedding-march pace, her sense of dignity choke-holding her panic. The central section of seats ended in a flat blank bulkhead. Behind it was a bank of lavatories, every one available. She picked the center door because it was the farthest from any sleeper, shut the accordion door, and shot home its tiny bolt. An overhead light came on, followed by an exhaust fan with a bad bearing. Danny found its rattle comforting. No one would hear her retching.

She bent over the stainless steel bowl, one sweaty hand on either plastic wall of the little compartment, and waited. And waited. And nothing came out of her but—after a full minute's trying—a sigh. She gave it up, turned to the toy sink, and ran some tepid water into her cupped hand. Above the sink was a tiny mirror and in the mirror her mother's face.

Not exactly her mother's face, which currently resided in Fort Lauderdale and was consequently very tanned, but one more and more like it every day. Dark and narrow—except at the forehead, which was wide enough, held apart by smooth black brows, the eyes beneath them almost as dark and almost as overlarge. Beneath those a nose that was nondescript by Furey standards and a small mouth whose lips were drawn now like a double bowstring.

Danny thought of an old saying: By forty every man has the face he deserves. Or was it thirty? Fifty? Damn. She was only certain that it was equally true of a woman. She had her mother's face and—no credit to her—it was the very one she deserved. A face to reprove her, to remind her of her sins, the few of commission and the sad many of omission.

Kerry the brother had the Furey face, which was largely the Furey nose, accompanied by small bright eyes, a dimpled chin, and wild hair; all gifts from their long dead father, along, it seemed, with his lifeline. An unpredictable and cheerful man, he'd been short-lived, so much so that Danny always fell back on memories of photographs when she tried to picture him.

Danny rubbed the waiting water into her face and patted it dry with a paper towel. The waste bin was crammed to bursting, so she folded the towel and held the damp square in her palm. She opened the lavatory door and jumped. A woman was standing there. An older woman with tannic skin, her head arched back so she could look up into Danny's face, her eyes darting blurs behind square glasses. Her whole look was questioning, almost entreating. What have you to say to me? Do you have some word for me? A message? An answer?

Danny was struck by the sudden certainty that she looked into every stranger's face the same way this old woman did, with the same silent supplication. She stammered an apology and stepped out of the doorway, noticing as the woman pushed past her that every other lavatory was still vacant.

Must like a warm seat, she told herself.

Beyond the last door and across the aisle was the skin of the plane and a window set well behind the last row of seats. Danny crossed to it, squeezing a shoulder between the edge of the window and a fire extinguisher. She placed the damp square of toweling against the plastic wall and held it there with her temple, though the impulse to be sick was now gone completely.

Because she was standing, her view was almost straight down. She could see scattered clouds thousands of feet below and, as far again beneath them, the Atlantic, its great rollers moonlit ripples. She imagined being tossed on those waves, the sole survivor of an air disaster, helpless and alone.

It was a bad habit of hers, imagining herself in some awful state just to evoke a hothouse anguish or despair. She was surprised to find now that the nightmare image of drowning alone, perhaps with a last glimpse of another airliner's lights passing high overhead, added nothing at all to the dread she was already feeling.

CHAPTER TWO

"Make your setting a springboard to conflict."
—*Camelot Guide to Romance Writing*

"So, which car are you drawn to, yourself?"

At the car rental counter in the Shannon Airport, Danny stood tapping a small foot while Kerry flirted with the agent and—almost as an afterthought—rented them a car. Kerry's current sallies involved cars that were attractive to women. He'd already exhausted the possibilities suggested by the agent's name: Rose. Was she from Tralee? Was she one of the wild Irish roses? As it was September, was there any chance of her being the last rose of Kerry's summer?

Danny was recognized only once, when the moment came to produce her driver's license so she could be listed as the alternate driver. Otherwise she was free to marvel at how easily Kerry got away with the flirtation.

Was it, Danny wondered, because the very young agent, whose ill-fitting blazer sleeves were always over her knuckles or being pushed out of the way, saw this thirty-nine-year-old man as ancient? Danny had overheard retirees saying amazing things to the counter help at the coffee shop where she sat every day with her laptop and wrote. This woman's tolerance couldn't be due to Kerry's illness; the signs—the slightest paleness of skin and hollowness of cheek—were barely visible to Danny. She finally attributed the clerk's patience to their being Americans and crazy by definition.

When the Fureys were alone in the lot with their car, a very red Ford sedan, Danny said, "This is way more car than we need."

Kerry shrugged. "Rose was a nice kid. I'm hoping she gets a commission."

"Rose. When did you become such a butthead with the opposite sex?"

"I've always been a butthead with the opposite sex. I've just been a silent butthead, like all Fureys. Now I say anything that comes into it. My head, I mean, not my butt. Or maybe I don't, since in correct psychological terms, I've gone from being anal retentive to anal dispersive."

"You're misusing anal retentive and making up anal dispersive."

"Coining it, you mean. It's my contribution to human knowledge. I was hoping to make one."

He strolled around to the left-hand door, the passenger door, which didn't surprise Danny. On their previous joint visit to Ireland, ten years behind them and still an open wound, Kerry had managed never once to get behind the wheel. If he hadn't been financing the current expedition—and if Rose hadn't been blonde and twenty-two—Kerry's name would never have appeared on the Ford's paperwork.

That infamous trip of 1998 had been a failure in all respects. The Fureys had failed to accomplish their dead father's lifelong but unattempted dream of visiting his own father's birthplace. They'd failed as well to reconcile with one another, to end the estrangement that had begun when Danny had left the family home to marry, leaving Kerry behind to care for their widowed mother. In fact, traveling together had been a source of new offenses and new injuries, which had taken on lives of their own.

The failure to visit their paternal grandfather's actual

birthplace had been due to a substitution in their family's oral history. They'd been taught that he'd come from Leenane, a small village in County Galway, which they'd dutifully found and photographed. But some time after their return to the States, they'd heard from a distant American relation who had done actual research on the family. He'd discovered that the Fureys had actually sprung from Letterfenny, a tiny mountain village, now deserted. Leenane was merely the closest town that appeared in any atlas. As such, it had somehow substituted itself for Letterfenny in the family's collective memory. Kerry had promptly sworn that he would someday find Letterfenny, and Danny that he would do it without her. But here she was.

She sighed and spread the rental agency's map on the sedan's roof, while Kerry, his back against his door, studied a gyring hawk high above the marshy ground beyond the nearest runway. Although there were puddles about, there was also sunshine, the only clouds the tattered remnants of a defeated front.

"We could make it as far as Leenane tonight," Danny said. "If we keep at it." Then she added, ending a silence that Kerry had declined to fill, "If you think all that driving might tire you out, we could stop in Galway for the night."

"How about Limerick?" Kerry asked.

"We're already in Limerick. Or almost. It's just a few miles down the road. In the wrong direction." In more than one sense, she added to herself.

Kerry rolled along the side of the car until he was facing his sister, his dimpled chin made more dimpled by the prop of the car's roof. "The thing is, I booked rooms for us there. It's a town we know."

"Too well," Danny said. "Just cancel them."

"I can't. I mean, I already paid for today. I paid for last night so we could get into them early today. I wasn't sure how I'd hold up during the flight and I was pretty sure you wouldn't sleep much. You bitched the whole way across last time, remember? Said you knew how the famine Irish had felt in the coffin ships. As close to sacrilege as I've ever heard you come."

"There wasn't any legroom."

"Yeah. That's what those whiny immigrants missed the most. Anyway, I arranged for us to get into the rooms early so we could catnap for a couple of hours. Then we can have dinner, make it an early night. Tomorrow we'll be acclimated. Acclimatized. Take your pick."

Danny had had secret visions of being in Letterfenny that same evening, of taking a few souvenir photos, stealing a rock from the tumbled wall of a cottage, and shaking hands with Kerry at last, perhaps with a tear or two and certainly a Guinness thrown in. Then back to the airport and home. She knew it was a hopeless schedule, even though it would stay light this far north until well after dinnertime, but she gave it up reluctantly. "How do we find these rooms?"

"I'll navigate. It'll be like old times."

This oblique reference to their last Ireland adventure was enough to kill the conversation. That and Danny's problems with the car, which had its steering wheel on the wrong side and required her to shift gears with her unskilled left hand. Kerry sat up straight and paid attention for the first few miles, saying "left" every time they turned a corner to remind his chauffeur which side of the road to use. When Danny grew comfortable enough to tell him to shut up, Kerry settled back in his seat.

"I brought your new one with me," he said. "*Beyond Forever.* Who dreams up these titles?"

"Camelot has a separate staff for that," Danny replied, naming the publishing house for which she wrote, by its own reckoning the second largest publisher of romance fiction in the English-speaking world.

"Made up of ex–greeting card writers?"

"Ex-journalists," Danny said. "You're all closet romantics."

"We're closet sentimentalists, not romantics. There's a difference, I think. And speaking of sentiment, while we're over here, we should do some research on *The Quiet Man*. For that book we're going to collaborate on. *The Fureys' Complete Quiet Man*."

"We won't be over here long enough."

Kerry ignored the bald statement of fact. "Did you watch it on St. Patrick's Day?"

With that question, the tension inside the sedan relaxed somewhat. Like men who could only interact by talking about sports, the Furey siblings were only comfortable together when the subject was old movies. And they were almost friends again when the old movie in question was *The Quiet Man,* John Ford's gift to the Irish Tourist Board, the story of an American boxer who reclaims his Irish birthplace and finds true love to boot.

"Of course," Danny said. "You?"

"More recently than that. So recently it would be unfair to challenge you to a game."

"Try me."

"Okay. How about great throws from the movie? And for the sake of political correctness, we'll eliminate John Wayne throwing Maureen O'Hara on the bed."

"Leave political correctness out of it," Danny replied, "or we'll have to burn the whole film. Great throws, huh? I'll start. Wayne throwing his courting derby across the field. Must sail half a mile. I always wonder how he gets it back."

"You would. I'll take Barry Fitzgerald throwing the cork from O'Hara's whiskey bottle over his shoulder."

"*You* would," Danny said. "O'Hara throwing the wash rag in Victor McLaglen's face—and getting it to stick."

"Good. McLaglen throwing Wayne's trench coat at the old man in the bar. It sticks on his face, too, by the way."

"The old man is John Ford's brother, Francis," Danny reminded him.

"We'll do brothers later. Or are you conceding the current topic?"

"No. Let's see. Ward Bond throwing his fishing rod into the stream. And then reaching in to pull it out without looking down."

" 'God help us!' " Kerry mimicked. "Good one. Especially good, since you've left me the ultimate throw in the movie: O'Hara throwing her dowry into the fire box of the old steam tractor. Game, set, and match, I believe."

"Game only," Danny said, but almost to herself. And then, more softly still, "God help us."

CHAPTER THREE

"Part One is a snare for your heroine—and for your readers."
—Camelot Guide to Romance Writing

The Linden Tree Hotel was a very small, very clean establishment on the Killaloe road, a few miles outside of Limerick. It was run by a Mrs. Musgrove, a former teacher who believed she had a God-given talent for dealing with drunks and American tourists. Her technique with both was to "brook no nonsense," to borrow her own words. It was a slogan so dear to her heart that many a foreign visitor to the Linden Tree had gone away thinking "brook no nonsense" was what "fáilte," the traditional Irish welcome cut into the mossy stone above the hotel's front door, actually meant.

For all that, Mrs. Musgrove took immediately to Kerry, who greeted her with a string of nonsense that included a description of their flight and a celebration of the beauty of County Limerick, though most of the ground they'd covered since leaving the airport had been in County Clare and he'd paid scant attention to that. Danny, Mrs. Musgrove's true soul mate, was all but ignored. She carried her bags and Kerry's up to their separate rooms, making several trips from the incredibly narrow car park, where she was reluctant to leave the Ford, insured though it was.

Afterward, despite the banging of pipes and doors and the mutter of traffic coming in through her open window, Danny slept and dreamt. She was married again in her dream, as often happened. When she'd actually been married and living in Ohio, she'd frequently dreamt that she was back in her parents' home in New Jersey. Now she was divorced and had her own place in her native "Garden State," but she spent much of her dreamtime outside Columbus with Max in the barn-like suburban home they'd shared.

She awoke after a few hours and struggled to stay awake, fearful that further napping would have her out of sync with Irish time for the rest of their visit. She used the toy shower in her attached bath, which was almost as small as her late airliner lavatory though more cheerfully appointed. The shower's spray came from a wall-mounted plastic box along with a variety of sounds: moans and groans and a grinding out of all proportion to the amount of heated water produced.

Clean and dressed and still less than awake, Danny decided to rouse her brother. While she walked the Linden Tree's slanting hallway, she flashed back to the hundreds of times she'd been delegated to awaken Kerry when they'd been children together. This attempt ended, as so many of those lost ones had, in frustration. Kerry had left his door unlocked, and Danny stuck her head inside and called to him.

"Don't bother me till breakfast is on the table," Kerry replied, his head beneath the covers. "And not the first seating, either."

"Dinner, you mean."

"*Breakfast*, I mean."

In the parlor, Mrs. Musgrove was watching a television program about the artificial insemination of cattle. Danny looked in long enough to identify the subject matter and then retreated outside.

The hotel sat on a corner formed by the busy road and a quiet country lane. Danny followed the lane, enjoying the sun, now a late afternoon sun but warm. As she walked, she tried to locate a bird whose call was a single note repeated again and again, a dozen times to a set. And she fell into thinking how like their previous visit to Ireland this one had already become.

She'd spent many an idle morning on that trip—it felt like morning now after her nap, though it was past tea time—spent them walking about while Kerry recovered from a night in the pubs. They'd learned early in the week that the Irish roads were difficult to take hung over, especially for a helpless passenger. Luckily Danny liked to walk and—a writer then as now—she'd been used to her own company. She'd filled a notebook with observations on the Irish countryside, material she'd hoped to use in a novel but had misplaced. She'd brought a similar notebook along on this trip, one she would have to hide from Kerry or he would fill it with rambling notes on *The Fureys' Complete Quiet Man* or some other even more unlikely project.

Half a mile down the road from the hotel, Danny came to the ruin of a tower that stood in a field, well guarded by grazing cows, black ones so shiny they might have been curried. She looked around for a historical marker before she remembered how rare those were in Ireland. In New Jersey, anything half as old as this tower, which was rectangular and nearly the height of the Linden Tree though sadly broken off, would have been a national monument. In this land of ruins, the nameless fragment of a fortified house was just a thing for the cows to contemplate.

Cows and solitary walkers. For on the far side of the pasture, on a lane that ran parallel to Danny's own, stood another admirer of antiquity, a lone woman. Due to the distance between them, the American could tell little about her, only that she wore a brown coat and had a blue scarf on her head, tied in the style of a countrywoman. Danny thought she might be young—despite her dated dress—but that was only an impression. The stranger was intent on the ruin, Danny decided, for there was nothing else in view save the cows and herself.

She started back, suddenly feeling uneasy again, as she had on the plane. It was their proximity to Limerick, she decided, the town where she and Kerry had had their principal falling-out in 1998, where the uneasy truce of that expedition had broken down completely, and she fell into thinking about that breakdown, almost against her will. On that visit, they'd stayed in a modern hotel in the shadow of Bunratty Castle, one not unlike an American motel, which Kerry had disliked for that reason.

Danny took to their dinner at Bunratty Castle about as well. Billed as a medieval banquet, it was as touristy as anything they'd done in Ireland. As touristy as anything one could do in Ireland, kissing the Blarney Stone included. A hundred diners, mostly other Americans, were herded into the banquet hall and seated on benches set at long bare tables. There they were given mead, served in earthenware cups filled from earthenware jugs, and entertained by an attractive chorus of young women—all dressed in medieval costume, long velvet dresses with satin sleeves, whose dark rich colors set off the wearers' pale complexions.

The master of ceremonies, also in costume, always appointed one of the tourists "earl for the evening." He selected another to be "the prisoner," a miscreant tossed into a cell off the main dining hall for comic relief. For this role, the emcee's practiced eye singled out Kerry from all the likely young men assembled that night. And he wasn't disappointed in his choice. Though Kerry had been sulking over their hotel until the moment of his selection, he played the part to the hilt and beyond, his plaintive cries of "more mead" interrupting the proceedings regularly. The reigning earl, a dentist from Louisiana, granted the request every time.

The Prisoner Furey finally won his release—as all his many

predecessors had—by singing a song for the assembled company. American prisoners almost always chose one of two songs, "My Wild Irish Rose" or "When Irish Eyes Are Smiling," both as authentically Irish as "Putting on the Ritz." Kerry surprised his hosts by selecting "Those Endearing Young Charms," and crooning it creditably. He was served dinner finally to hearty applause.

Through all of this, Danny had sat like a prisoner herself, a condemned one. She'd been befriended by an unescorted lady from New York City, who—though older and blessed with broad heavy features—had been pleasant enough company. The New Yorker had been to the dinner before and she'd explained its immutable steps to Danny, often before they occurred. She'd warned her specifically about the mead, fermented honey that went down smoothly but "really kicks your ass."

There had been no way to pass those warnings on to the incarcerated Kerry. He'd seemed steady upon his release, but he'd also developed a definite taste for the mead. While Danny had pushed food his way, the other diners had shared their mead jugs like lost relations. By the time the revels ended at dusk, Kerry's ass had been well and truly kicked.

Danny came out of her memories with the feeling of someone's eyes upon her. She looked to her right, to the parallel lane, and there was the woman in the brown coat, matching her step for step. The stranger's eyes were on the road before her, but Danny had the strong impression that she had just looked away. As she watched, the woman disappeared behind a hedgerow without a backward glance.

CHAPTER FOUR

"Back-story can back up your story. Use as little as possible."
—Camelot Guide to Romance Writing

Danny arrived back at the Linden Tree and to the present awake enough to be hungry. Unfortunately, Kerry hadn't thought to order dinner for them, and the hotel's small dining room was completely booked. After looking in on Kerry and receiving no encouragement—indeed, no answer—Danny set out to walk the short distance along the main road to the restaurant where Mrs. Musgrove was sending her overflow.

The walk took her away from Limerick proper, but she felt no easier for that, deep as she was in memories of Bunratty Castle. The restaurant, the Thorn Stick, diverted her momentarily, being a husband-and-wife operation run on cat-and-dog lines, the proprietors arguing steadily and theatrically as they cooked and served. The bull-necked man and the pale, plump woman seemed unable to stay in the same room together. When one entered the restaurant proper, the other would run into the kitchen, predicting the certain demise of the food in progress, the entire operation, and the marriage in very clear tones.

Danny therefore grew genuinely concerned when the two met in the center of the main room, not far from her table. This seemed a calamity on the order of matter meeting antimatter, and she braced herself for an explosion. Instead, she and the other customers received a song, an old one, "The Raven and the Rose," beautifully harmonized.

After the last note had faded, the two flew apart again, restoring the natural balance of the Thorn Stick and perhaps the universe itself. But Danny did not relax. The song had reminded her again of the banquet at Bunratty, might in fact have been one she'd heard there. She'd no sooner had that thought than she spotted the old castle in a photograph on the dining room wall. Then in another and another. In a fourth frame she saw the castle's pub, where Kerry had retired after the banquet to first distinguish and then disgrace himself.

The mystery was explained by her hostess, who was gesturing toward yet another photo while accepting a compliment on her singing. This one was a group portrait of the Bunratty performers in their medieval finery. They were the cast of an earlier era, Danny realized, spotting the wife—a younger, slimmer version of the wife—in the center of the group.

Her hostess could easily have been one of the singers Danny had heard ten years before, a thought that yanked the American back to that night despite all her efforts to resist. While she ate her overcooked beef and potatoes and watched the Limerick-Killaloe traffic through the little restaurant's storefront windows, she remembered her efforts to get the drunken Kerry to their motel after the medieval banquet. As she relived it, she felt the same sense of impending doom she'd felt that night.

The master of ceremonies' closing remarks had included recommendations for the castle's "folk park" and for its pub, Durty Nelly's. Kerry had made a beeline for the latter, "beeline" being no idle word choice, for he was after more fermented honey. Danny chose the folk park, a recreation of a pre-industrial Irish village, complete with craft demonstrations aided, as the sun disappeared, by very industrial electric lights. She watched those demonstrations from a distance, never straying far from the village's circular path for fear an actor playing a weaver or a potter would address her.

When the park closed finally, Danny went to the pub—itself a tourist attraction but crowded with authentic local drinkers—and found Kerry leading a Beatles sing-along, a glass in hand. The pint glass had been intended by its designer to hold beer, but it was half full of mead, the sight of which caused Danny to despair. She trudged back to her room and fell asleep reading in a chair.

She awoke well after one, certain that Kerry had not returned. Sure enough, his unlocked room was empty. She returned to Durty Nelly's, where she found that Kerry was still the center of the floor show, though the music had given way to comedy: unconfined laughter at the expense of the royally drunk American.

Danny had led her staggering brother back to the hotel, where Kerry had been sick and sick again. The resulting epic hangover had blighted what remained of their week together, their flight to New York, and their all but wordless good-bye at JFK. And now they were within a mile or two of that same pub.

Danny mulled that over as she walked back to the Linden Tree, pondering, too, her brother's earlier disinterest in a landscape they'd come three thousand miles to see. By the time she reached the hotel, the novelist had convinced herself that the disinterest had been an act, intended by Kerry to lull his sister's fears of Limerick. The conclusion quickened both her pace and her pulse.

Once inside, Danny climbed to Kerry's room and tried the door. It was still unlocked. And the form still lay beneath the blankets on the bed, just visible now that only evening light remained to challenge the paper window shades.

Then Danny called to her brother, and the act of addressing the shape in the bed broke the spell. She saw that it hadn't moved since her last look-in and that it was too small by far, missing as it was any suggestion of legs or feet. She crossed to the bed and pulled back the blankets, revealing pillows, carelessly arranged.

Downstairs Mrs. Musgrove was making change for a departing customer, her slow movements as she counted it out perfectly suited to the ponderous size of the European coinage.

"Your brother?" she asked when Danny had succeeded in gaining her notice. "He left an hour ago and more. Asked for a ride to Bunratty Castle. I was happy to find him one, though I told him he'd get there too late for the show."

"It won't start without him," Danny assured her.

Chapter Five

"Is your heroine looking for love or just looking for the exit?"
—Camelot Guide to Romance Writing

Durty Nelly's was larger than the pub of Danny's memories. And less subterranean. She remembered descending a stairway into a room well below the level of the thoroughfare, a low-ceilinged, ill-lit room. As she entered the real pub—down a single worn step from the sidewalk—she wondered why she'd subconsciously darkened the place and shrunk it. The lighting was certainly as generous as any American tavern's. Though the pub was crowded, Danny had no trouble picking Kerry out from the doorway. For once her brother had chosen a quiet table well away from the center of the room. And for the moment he was alone.

Kerry looked up with mild surprise when Danny's shadow fell on him, surprise mixed with pleasure, as though an old acquaintance had happened upon him. "Sis, great. Join me."

He extended the chair opposite his own with an unseen foot. Like the table, the chair had been roughly made of some yellow wood. Together they reminded Danny of a school desk from some forgotten grade.

Danny sat down heavily and leaned toward Kerry's drink, a colorless liquid in a glass that might once have held a votive candle. "No mead tonight?"

Kerry shivered. "Mead? I still can't stand the smell of that

33

stuff. It was years before I could eat honey on a bagel. Did you expect to find me drunk again? Maybe wearing my jeans as a hat?"

"Why did you come here?"

"I dunno. I felt drawn to the place. I've been thinking a lot about my life lately, as you'll understand. The last night I was here always stands out for me. I took a turning that night or missed a step or something. I wish I could remember it better. Maybe a beautiful woman gave me her number and I lost it."

"Maybe," Danny said. A further something seemed to be in order, so she asked, "What's that you're drinking?"

Kerry's smile became genuine, which is to say, his small eyes joined in with it, crinkling at their corners. "Poteen. Irish white lightning. Unlicensed and strictly illegal. The guy who drove me over from the hotel happened to mention that he knew a guy who knew a guy. I've always wanted to try it.

"Remember Uncle Jack bringing that bottle back with him when we were little? And how he wouldn't share it with Dad, his own brother? That kind of selfishness creates a mystique. I decided right then there had to be something to the stuff. So I couldn't pass up a chance to buy a bottle."

He reached down and lifted something from the floor at his feet. The neck of a bottle appeared above the table and then disappeared again.

"They're letting you drink that in here?"

"Not officially. I struck a deal with one of the barmen. I've a way with bartenders and waitresses."

One of the latter group appeared at their table as though on cue, a frazzled woman who'd spent too many nights in smoke-filled rooms like this one. She smiled at Danny when she asked her her pleasure, revealing a gap in her upper teeth where a canine had once resided.

"She'll have a Furey special," Kerry said. "And I'll have

another. Better bring her a Guinness, too."

"A real one, darling?" the woman asked.

"Yes, thanks."

Watching her go, Kerry emptied his little glass with a sigh. "Maybe she's the one who gave me her number ten years ago. Maybe I was supposed to save her from a life of cigarette smoke and home dentistry."

Danny repeated a question she'd first asked on the 747 over the ocean: "Should you be drinking at all? With your medications, I mean."

"Who knows? It might even help. This poteen might help, I mean. Maybe it's the wonder drug everybody is searching for, one of the secret cures we're supposed to be losing because we're cutting down all the rain forests. Only the ingredients to this one weren't in the rain forests, they were here, in Ireland, which, come to think of it, was probably the first rain forest that ever got mowed."

He was babbling them far from the original question, and Danny was content to let him. All their lives they'd handled the big subjects this way: with feints and quick retreats.

The waitress returned carrying a pint of stout drawn by a master and two empty glasses that matched the one Kerry handed her with a wink. When she'd gone, he poured two drinks and returned the bottle, square and squat and unlabeled, to the floor.

"To your very good health," he said, quoting *The Quiet Man* again and without irony.

Danny examined her portion briefly before following her brother's example and drinking off about half. "Like vodka," she said, her voice a husk. "Cheap, warm vodka."

"That's what I thought after the first one. After the third, I started to recognize certain twists and turns that vodka lacks. Extra beats to the measure, you might say. Now I see it's an altogether more complicated experience."

"I'll take your word for it." Danny slid the poteen Kerry's way and claimed the pint of Guinness. A single sip brought her voice back to something like normal. "You've paid for how many of those empty glasses?"

Kerry shrugged. "They're running a tab."

"Come back to the hotel and drink it for free."

"I'm paying for the atmosphere, Sis." He indicated the noisy room in total with a sweep of his arm. "And for the company. Speaking of which, here comes somebody I want you to meet."

Danny saw him coming toward them through the maze of tables, a tall redhead dressed in the staff's uniform of white shirt, its sleeves rolled back, and black jeans, his gray in the knees from wear. He was looking about the room from under slightly lowered brows and through a few stray red hairs. A look reminiscent of Mortensen playing Aragorn, and probably, Danny decided, lifted from Mortensen. This strider was in search of empty glasses, which he added to the trove he carried on a large tray, effortlessly. In this, he had leverage on his side, being rangy, as true redheads so often are.

"Hey Frank! This is my sister, Danny. Danny, this is Francis O'Shea."

"Danny?" the newcomer asked, placing his tray on the table's edge and holding it there with one faded knee. "Short for?"

"Danielle," Kerry said. "We tried using that from time to time. It never seemed to fit her."

Danny might have told him that herself, but she was somewhat wordless. Words were the stuff of her profession and words describing the moment when a man and woman meet were her specialty, cute or unusual meetings being a requirement for all Camelot books. This particular meeting, in a smoky pub, would have been rejected out of hand by her editor, unless of course there'd been some earlier inkling. If, for example, this

Frank O'Shea had been the figure she'd glimpsed during her afternoon walk and not the woman in the blue scarf. Then this second—

Danny cut herself off, realizing that she was hiding from the moment. She focused on the smiling face gazing down on her expectantly, forcing herself to meet his eyes, his truly magnificent blue eyes. His face was not without a few boyish freckles—only a few, though the abundant red hair, worn just over his ears, made those few glow on his flat cheeks and across his quite ordinary nose, smallish and ever so square at the tip.

Kerry was rambling on. "Frank's the one who worked out my arrangement regarding the poteen. I told him about the special place this pub has in our family history." Here Danny winced almost imperceptibly. "Were you here ten years ago, Frank?"

"God no. I was in Berlin, raising hell."

"I'll bet. We boys got to talking and found out we have a lot in common. He dropped out of college to care for an aging mother, too." Danny winced again. "Afterward, he lived in Boston for a while."

"Till my visa expired," the barman said with a shrug. "So you're the novelist, then."

Danny glanced at Kerry with as much admiration as irritation, the admiration for the speed with which her brother worked, the irritation for the work itself.

"Just a storyteller, really," she said, falling back on the modest claim she always used at the beginning of talks to library groups and schoolchildren.

"*Just* a storyteller?" Frank repeated. "Be careful who you say that to. You're in the land of storytellers now. We have novelists for breakfast."

Kerry laughed and Danny smiled, though it might actually have been her third wince. She decided to change the subject. "How did you like America?" she asked, a trace of the poteen burr back in her voice.

"I liked it fine, what I saw. Though I never got used to the straight answers."

"The straight answers?" Kerry prompted helpfully.

"Sure. You ask a question in Boston and you'll get a straight answer, nine times out of ten. You can go months in Ireland and not hear one."

"We'll keep that in mind," Kerry said.

"Do that. It was grand meeting you," he said to Danny.

The storyteller was preoccupied with the movement of Frank's white shirt across his broad shoulders as he hefted his tray. So preoccupied in fact that her "and you" was late coming out. It bounced off Frank's back as he collected empty glasses at the next table.

"Drink up," Kerry said, smiling at her. "I'm sure we're late for something."

CHAPTER SIX

"Your heroine may not believe in love at first sight,
but you have to."
—*Camelot Guide to Romance Writing*

Danny was unable to sleep upon their return to the Linden
Tree. She finally dropped off around two, just after a gentle rain
had begun to patter down. Predictably she overslept, not wak-
ing until the rain deserted her at half past eight. When she
finally descended, hurrying, to the dining room, she found
Kerry wiping the last trace of grease from his breakfast plate
with a crust of toast.

Kerry up and dressed and fed at that hour was a minor
miracle, one Danny attributed to the younger Furey's having
missed his dinner. Despite the absence of physical evidence, she
knew her brother's plate had contained a "full Irish breakfast":
eggs, black pudding, grilled tomato, bacon, and bangers, that
nose-on name for sausages. Kerry had never missed the chance
to have one on their previous trip. The feast also included the
aforementioned white toast, one piece of which still stood in a
silver wire rack designed to hold four slices upright and well
apart.

"Remember these things?" Kerry asked, waving the rack like
a dinner bell. "We called them 'Irish Toast Coolers, guaranteed
to prevent household accidents caused by warm toast.' "

"I remember." Danny sat down on the opposite side of the

39

little table Kerry had secured in a sunny—for the moment—corner of the dining room. "No headache this morning?"

"Not a trace. That poteen may actually be a wonder drug."

"Great. We can make it to Leenane today if the rain's gone for good."

"That may be a little ambitious," Kerry said. Then he beamed at the waitress who arrived to take Danny's order—muesli—and deliver a fresh pot of coffee.

"Galway, then," Danny said, feeling as though they were back were they'd begun, trapped in the airport car park. To break that spell, she added a new proposition. "We can go by the Cliffs of Moher. It's out of our way, but we can still make Galway by dinnertime if we start right now."

Kerry was playing with the toast cooler again, moving the surviving piece of bread from slot to slot. "What can we make if we start at, say, noon?"

Danny set down her coffee cup. "If you've already paid for rooms somewhere, knock off the byplay and tell me."

"It isn't that. I screwed up. Forgot one of my medications. We left so quick, and I'm taking so many. Anyway, Mrs. Musgrove helped me put a call through to my doctor back home. He wasn't too pleased to hear from me, by the way, since it was two in the morning over there. I actually enjoyed spoiling *his* sleep for a change. Anyway, he's faxing over the prescription to a pharmacist in Limerick. A chemist, Mrs. M called him. But it'll be noon before everything's straightened out. Sorry. We can keep the rooms till one, I checked."

The person who had granted this dispensation bustled in before Danny could officially acquiesce. The landlady nodded to her before addressing her pet. "I have that chemist on the line again. He has some insurance questions for you."

"See you upstairs, Sis," Kerry said, leaving Danny to chew her twiggy cereal and brood.

When she climbed again to the second floor, she found Kerry's room unlocked as always but empty. Entering her own room, Danny discovered her brother seated at a little table under the window, paging through her journal.

"Did I forget to lock this?" Danny asked, shutting the door a little firmly.

"Wouldn't be like you to," Kerry replied without getting up. "I did an article for the paper last year on lock picking. Took some lessons from a real pro. I still practice whenever I can. Opening that lock there was less trouble than turning the knob. I used this, in fact." He held up a stiff and glossy brochure. "Found it in a rack by Mrs. Musgrove's phone. Thought you might be interested."

Danny took the pamphlet, noting first the end that had been creased when Kerry had slipped back her bolt and then the subject matter: King John's Castle in Limerick proper.

Kerry was still absently fingering the journal's pages. "They've made a lot of progress with the castle since we were here ten years ago, but it's still more of an archeological dig than a tourist trap. I remembered you missed seeing it when we last passed through. You could drive us into town and take the tour."

"Are you up to climbing battlements?"

"Me? No. I wasn't thinking of doing it myself. I have to pick up my prescription. And there's some other shopping I want to do."

Danny rescued the notebook, slipping it back into her suitcase. She sat down on the bed next to Kerry's chair, the proximity calculated to pin her brother in place. "What shopping? What are you up to now?"

The other Furey nodded happily, as though Danny had made a particularly clever move in some game they were playing.

"It's the poteen," Kerry said. "I can't be sure of finding

another source up north. I want to lay in a bottle or two before we go. I'd take you along, but it's strictly a Joe-sent-me kind of deal. You might make the guy nervous. He's certain to make you nervous. Plus, if the place is raided and we're both there, who'll bail us out?"

Further equally plausible reasons were forthcoming, but Danny cut them off with a raised hand. "Fine. I'll do the castle. I just wanted the truth."

"It's all the truth, Sis," Kerry assured her, jerking a thumb toward the bright world beyond the window as he got up from his chair. "It's what you make of it that counts. And remember, I said it."

They drove into the city, Danny fussy again behind the wheel after a layoff of only a night. Kerry navigated using directions written out by Mrs. Musgrove on the backs of a half a dozen little telephone message slips, which he shuffled noisily until Danny threatened to throw them all out the window, "all" meaning Kerry as well. Near Bunratty Castle, they overtook a lone runner with a long, loose stride.

"That's Frank, isn't it?" Kerry said. "It is. Pull over so we can say hello."

To Danny's surprise, her hands were turning the wheel and her foot braking while her mind was still marshalling her objections.

They came to rest beyond the runner, who loped up to Danny's open window.

"Lost already?" he asked.

Danny was on the verge of asking him if he'd had any novelists for breakfast. Luckily, Kerry cut her off.

"Not us," he said, holding up his yellow slips. "We have directions."

"All of those? Are you off to Buenos Aires?"

"Limerick," Danny managed to say. "King John's Castle."

"You'd better let me drive you. You can buy me lunch."

Blue eyes or no blue eyes, this was too much for Danny, a woman who said no first and asked herself questions later. "We wouldn't want to take up your time."

"I've nothing but time," Frank replied. He added, almost as an afterthought, "Thanks to this brother of yours. Our deal about the poteen came to the attention of my boss at the pub. I've been discharged. Don't trouble yourselves about it. It's not a job I'll dream about in years to come."

He opened Danny's door. "Now, if you don't mind riding in the back, I promise to get you there safe."

Danny was in the back and struggling with her seatbelt before she'd thought of the rental car company and what they'd make of an unlisted driver, in the event of an accident. Finding out seemed to her a real possibility once they reached Limerick proper and Frank began to weave his way through its traffic while Kerry distracted him by waving his yellow slips and demanding to be let off at his chemist's.

The chemist's! Danny had forgotten their plan to split up. "We should stay together," she said in panic as they grounded against the chemist's curb. "We can come back here after lunch."

"Nonsense," Kerry replied with something of Mrs. Musgrove's authority. "See you at the Cock and Bull at noon sharp."

Then he was gone, and they were away before Danny could shift herself to the front seat. Frank began to describe their destination in such detail that Danny thought at first he was trying to put her at ease and then that he might actually be steadying himself.

"You can see King John's Castle there already. It's a rare one in any land: a castle whose walls are largely intact, whose keep and towers haven't been yanked down by assaulting armies or picked apart by scavenging stone masons. It's always seemed less romantic to me for that. Businesslike, you might say. Contemporary, even."

This suggestion was reinforced for Danny by the neighborhood around the castle, whose red brick row homes crowded right up to the massive walls. Frank parked on one of the narrow side streets that dead-ended at the Shannon River. Danny left the car without the usual sense she had at the end of an Irish drive—the sense of having cheated death. Instead, she felt the hot discomfort of being on a blind date.

And a date with an underdressed man at that, Frank being attired in a once-black track suit. He unzipped the jacket slightly and remussed his long hair and appeared content. Certainly he was no more informal than the younger half of the tour group they joined.

They followed it from one of the castle's restored rooms to the next. Their guide, a bespectacled young man, had a philosophical turn of mind and discussed the massive pile of stone not as a machine of war but as the eponymous regent's way of cheating death, of keeping his name—cursed though it was on Irish shores—alive.

Danny recognized a kinship with King John in this desire to be remembered. She had often imagined the day when her own bad news would be announced to her by some indifferent doctor. In these daydreams, she used the time remaining to her to set aside her romance novels and write a "real book," one that would survive.

Now, as she passed her nose above display cases holding the scant gleanings of the long archeological dig—bits of mail, spear points, a rusted iron glove—she felt a cold despair radiating around her. Felt it for King John and his dead knights certainly, but also for herself.

It was a relief, then, when, after the formal tour had ended, Frank suggested a return to the battlements for the view they afforded of the Shannon and the living hills beyond. These were modest cultivated hills, but lit bright by passing breaks in the overcast, and their green was the breath-catching true green of Ireland. True not as to shade, there being many, but in intensity.

"They were here before the castle," Frank said of the hills. "And they'll be here when it's finally gone and King John forgotten."

Danny thought how odd it was that this stranger should address her unspoken thoughts and that they should be leaning shoulder-to-shoulder against the battlements without awkwardness or at least without terrible awkwardness. His voice was lilting to her New World ear, its risings and fallings invoking a subliminal stir in her as strong as that produced by the green hills. Then she became aware of a less pleasant sensation, that of being watched.

Danny turned from the view and saw her again, the woman in the brown coat whose afternoon stroll had coincided with Danny's own the previous day. She was standing near the doorway of the nearest tower, no more than twenty yards away, her blue head scarf glistening like the river in a patch of sunlight. Danny was able to confirm her earlier guess regarding the woman's age—she was certainly not yet twenty—and also her parting impression that this stranger had been observing her. She was certainly studying Danny now, though as soon as the American caught her eye, she turned and entered the tower.

"I've an old friend here," Danny said to Frank. She went on to describe the woman who'd paced her walk the afternoon before.

"You'll often see the same people while visiting a little place like Limerick," Frank replied. "In fact, when I worked one summer driving tourists up and down the west coast in a little van, I found we were bumping into the same groups over and over again as we made the rounds. The other guides and I would try to stagger our schedules, so our charges wouldn't feel like they were going from one room to the next of a museum in one long queue, but there was only so much we could do. Ireland's a small country, after all."

He consulted his watch. "Time to meet the brother."

He led her to the winding staircase the woman in brown had just entered. Danny worked up an opening remark to use in case they overtook the stranger on the stairs or in the courtyard below. But they found both empty.

CHAPTER SEVEN

"One good twist deserves another."
—*Camelot Guide to Romance Writing*

On the short drive to the Cock and Bull, Danny felt the strain of being alone with this stranger returning. She was in the front seat now, no closer than she'd been to him on the castle's battlements but without the endless view and open sky. To combat this loss of visual space, she thought of making small talk, but it was a thing for which she had neither talent nor practice. There were two weightier subjects ready to hand, the ones between which her mind had been traveling back and forth like a shuttlecock between two racquets: Kerry's illness and the upcoming hunt for Letterfenny. She seized on the latter as the less indiscreet and gave Frank a brief outline.

"I could help with that," he said casually. "I've hiked the hills out there many times. There are some grand trails above Killary Harbor. I've probably even seen this Letterfenny. I've happened on many a lonely ruin, often by a spring. That country's alive with springs."

Danny had an inspiration and spoke it aloud before she could have a second thought. "You should come with us. I mean, we could hire you. You said you've worked as a tour guide. It wouldn't be a long job, but you'd be helping us out."

"You'd be helping me out, you mean. But I could give you a hand with your brother, in case he feels poorly."

"How did you know about that?"

"Kerry mentioned it last night in the pub. He has a gift for autobiography, your brother."

"Then you'll do it?"

"I will."

She sat in silence for the short remainder of the drive, frightened by her initiative and happy over it as well, happy that for once she'd be surprising Kerry. It was just after noon when they arrived at the Cock and Bull, a pub built before electric light and not much improved, Danny decided, by its invention. Coming in from the sunny street, it took her a moment to adjust her eyes to the twilight of the place. She scanned the tables for Kerry and missed him, looking as she was for a solitary figure. Then her eye was caught by Kerry's signalman's wave and by another, more restrained one. And he saw that her brother had a companion at his table and that the companion was someone she knew almost as well: her ex-husband, Max Alnutt.

For the merest second, Danny attributed Max's presence in the Cock and Bull to wild coincidence. Then Kerry's expression of more than total innocence made cobwebs of the idea. Before she could demand an explanation, Max was out of his chair and enveloping her in both a familiar bear hug and a fog of Armani cologne.

"Kerry didn't tell you I was coming," Max rumbled in his basso monotone. "Typical."

Max next shook hands with Frank, who had been hanging back politely. Danny noted that the two men were of a height, though she'd never heard anyone call Max, the linebacker who had left the cartilage of both knees on the playing field of Ohio Stadium, rangy.

Kerry, who'd made a show of standing but actually hadn't, said, "Frank, this is my ex-brother-in-law Max. Danny's ex, I should say. Max, this is Frank O'Shea. Danny and I met him last night. Got him fired last night, I should say."

"You got him fired, you should say," Danny returned.

"He's a fast worker," Max said to Frank, with a nod at Kerry. "He got me kicked out of a gentlemen's club the first time I met him."

That voice, Danny thought. It had once fascinated her but now seemed to her emblematic of Max's general phoniness. She remembered one of their Halloweens together when he'd gone to a party as Elvis Presley and spent the evening crooning, "Thank you very much," to everyone with barely a change in his day-to-day intonation.

"Gentlemen's Club?" Frank asked.

"Strip joint," Kerry said. "It was his bachelor party. I—"

"Never mind that," Danny snapped. "Let's jump ahead to today's story."

"Certainly," Kerry said. "But have a seat."

Both Frank and Max reached to pull out Danny's chair. She settled the matter by pulling one out for herself.

"Get your prescription?" she asked as she sat down.

From out of his blazer's distended right pocket, Kerry pulled a brown pill bottle. He shook it, but it made no noise, being full and stopped with cotton. He started to put it away. Then, smiling, he held it out so Danny could read the chemist's name and address from its paper label.

"And the poteen?"

This question Kerry answered with his foot, tapping what sounded like a paper bag containing at least two bottles.

"So we haven't just been waiting for Max to arrive?"

"Not entirely," Kerry said.

"Why wasn't he on our flight yesterday? Don't tell me he couldn't get a seat. I remember some empty ones."

"I flew out of Cleveland," Max said. Then, without losing his salesman's smile, he owned up. "Kerry was afraid you wouldn't get on the plane if you saw me at JFK. He called me the other night and told me about his condition and about this trip."

"We've stayed in touch," Kerry explained. "Christmas cards, e-mails—"

"Conspiracies."

"Kerry thought you might need a hand over here, if the traveling got to be too much for him. And I've always wanted to see Ireland. I make most of my living from it, after all."

"The waiter said the shepherd's pie is good," Kerry interjected, interjecting himself as well, thrusting his head and shoulders into the sight line between his sister and Max. "That's hard to believe, though. I mean, with a name like shepherd's pie, how good could it be? Shepherds weren't exactly at the top of the social pyramid, were they? If you heard something was called stableman's soufflé or chimneysweep's casserole, your mouth wouldn't start watering. You'd check the list of ingredients."

The man who had made the suspect recommendation arrived with pad and pencil in hand. Danny ordered a pint of stout and the shepherd's pie, almost saying stableman's soufflé by mistake. Max doubled that order as though congratulating her on her judgment. Frank asked for a bacon sandwich and tea and Kerry a bowl of potato soup.

"I've already made arrangements for help," Danny said when the man had gone off. "Frank's agreed to go with us as driver and guide."

"Has he?" Kerry asked.

To Danny's irritation, her brother wasn't the least bit put out. Max was, though he only showed it with an additional narrowing of his always narrow eyes.

"But I'm here now, Danielle."

Danny decided that the obvious fact required no confirmation, which left a gap in the conversation.

To fill it, perhaps, Frank asked Max, "How are you making your living from Ireland?"

"I'm a salesman. I work for a liquor distributor. We're the exclusive Midwest distributor for Curraghmore Cream, the liqueur. I can't tell you how many dollars of commissions I've made from that stuff."

I can tell you how many he's spent, Danny thought. *Every one he made and that much again.*

She had only recently paid off her half of the resulting debt, five years after their divorce, and was sensitive on the subject. She was sensitive, too, to the fact that Max was better dressed than she, in wrinkle-free travel clothes from the best catalog, and somehow more rested.

Another woman might have complained of those injustices aloud. Danny contented herself with glowering at the pint of Guinness now set before her, a hastily drawn thing, its head roiling like a nuclear cloud.

CHAPTER EIGHT

"What's better than trouble with a man?
Trouble with three men."
—Camelot Guide to Romance Writing

The food arrived shortly afterward, the pub's cook being as precipitate as its bartender. The Fureys and their guests treated the plates and bowls like strangers at the table. That is, they acted afraid to speak of personal things in front of them, retreating into general talk and—in Danny's case—silence.

Max turned the conversation, as he turned most conversations, to his beloved fishing. To Danny's relief, Frank was not a fellow worshipper at that shrine, though that didn't end the exchange but rather turned it into a lengthy monologue, much of it devoted to Max's recent pilgrimage to the trout streams of Montana.

While listening or pretending to, Kerry picked out a few chunks of potato from his soup and then pushed the bowl away. Then, while Max was taking a break for stout, he spoke to no one in particular.

"I've been thinking a lot about immortality recently." He started to reach for the paper sack at his feet, looked around the crowded pub, and helped himself to Danny's foamy pint instead. "I've been thinking that what I really want isn't to live for another twenty years. I want to live forever.

"It came to me in the wee small hours just after Dr. Metzler gave me the bad news. I'd started watching old movies that evening to calm myself down. *Chariots of Fire, Local Hero, The Quiet Man,* of course. It was my big gun. I didn't pop it into the DVD player until it got to be two and I still couldn't sleep.

"It hit me during the scene after the wedding. John Wayne is leaning back against a chest or a table in the parlor of his little cottage, thinking. Probably about having sex with his new bride, Maureen O'Hara. She hasn't locked him out of the bedroom yet, so everything is peaceful. And dark, the room lit only by the fire in the hearth."

"I'm with you," Danny said.

"He lights a cigarette. He reaches up and strikes the match against one of the cottage timbers, not looking at it, just staring off into the corner of the room. How many times do you figure we've watched him strike that match?"

"Too many," Max said, though softly.

"Too right. Watching it that night—that morning—I thought, 'That match is going to live longer than I am. Even if the leukemia crawls along and I get my twenty years. That match was struck in 1951, it burned for one or two seconds, and a hundred years from now it will still be around.' " He sighed. "Doesn't seem fair somehow."

The waiter chose that moment to arrive carrying a dessert menu. He took one look at their long faces and slunk away.

Kerry waved at his departing back and then addressed Frank and Max as he stood. "I'll just catch that guy and settle our bill. If I'm not mistaken, my sister will seize this opportunity for a private word with me."

Danny, who had been on the point of rising herself, sat back stubbornly, muttered a curse, and took off in pursuit. She caught up with Kerry at the bar, where he was pushing banknotes at the fugitive waiter.

"What were you thinking?" she demanded. "How could you

ask Max here without telling me?"

"As Max said himself, it wouldn't have worked any other way."

Refusing the offer of change, Kerry led Danny to a quieter end of the bar.

"I didn't want to tell you this in front of Max, but he and Lola have broken up. He got in touch with me before any of this started, asking how you were. I think he's feeling pretty low. When I got the idea for this trip, I thought it might be a way to get him out of himself."

"Good luck with that project."

Kerry was examining a grimy window. "Raining again. And the sun was out when I came in here."

"I know the feeling," Danny said.

Kerry patted her arm. "It'll all work out. Now, it looks like you've another appointment, so I'll visit the gents."

Danny turned and saw Max hovering nearby. He smiled when she met his eye. "You haven't changed," he said.

"Yes, I have," Danny said, but she made herself smile when she said it.

Perhaps she smiled too much. Max stepped closer and dropped his voice. "Lose this Frank guy."

"Excuse me?"

"I mean, thank him for the offer and all. And give him something for his time. But if you want me to help Kerry out—and I want to, don't get me wrong, he's a great guy—Frank's gotta go.

"And speaking of that, is the men's room this way?"

Tongue-tied, Danny watched him stride off. Then she retreated to the street, where she found Frank sheltering from the rain beneath the pub's patched awning.

"Taken up with Max where you left off?" he asked with a soft laugh. "Sorry, but your color is up. It suits you, by the way.

Look, if you're about to tell me that I'm fired before I even started, it's no problem."

"You don't want to come?"

"I do. A trip right now would be a godsend for me, but I'm not even sure I could go."

"If there's someone you need to ask . . ." *Some woman,* she added to herself.

"No, nothing like that. I mean, there's someone I could ask, should ask, but he'd say no. It's my boss at Durty Nelly's, a bruiser named Harty Doan."

"Your boss? I thought you'd been fired. Why would he care what you did?"

"I owe him some money. That is, a mate of mine, Barry, owes him a gambling debt, but I cosigned the marker so Harty wouldn't break Barry's legs. I was paying it off out of my wages, but now that I'm fired, Harty wants the rest in a lump and right away."

"Let Barry pay him."

"He ran off to Liverpool. Harty doesn't intend for that to happen again. So I don't think he'd fancy me going off with you."

"How does he expect you to pay him if you can't take a job when it comes along?"

Frank shrugged and for once omitted to brush the stray corkscrews of red hair from his eyes. "I don't know that he does. I think he's missing the chance he had to break a leg or two."

A yellow dog trotted up to them, its wet fur standing up in random clumps like ruined carpeting. The animal came within arm's reach, but backed away warily when Frank stooped to touch it. The novelist, who had lately identified with a dead king, now felt a sad affinity for this stray, which continued to watch them from a safe distance.

She came to a decision. "How soon can you be ready to go?"

"I'm ready now. If you insist on me shifting my clothes now and then, add an hour for packing. But what about Mr. Alnutt's feelings?"

"I stopped worrying about those when I stopped being Mrs. Alnutt."

He handed her the keys to the sedan. "I'm staying at my aunt's farm. It's in the shadow of a round tower on the Killaloe road. Your landlady can write you up some more yellow slips. In one hour."

Then he was off at a trot down the wet pavement. The yellow dog watched him go and then turned its wolf's head back to Danny.

"Fancy a trip?" she asked.

The rover shook off old rain to make room for new and pattered off toward the invisible river.

CHAPTER NINE

*"At the end of Part One, your heroine must decide to enter a
'Passageway of Destiny,' from which there is no return."*
—*Camelot Guide to Romance Writing*

It was a very quiet car that left the Linden Tree Hotel nearly an
hour later. Max, seated in the back with crossed arms, was
contributing most of the silence and had been since Danny announced her decision to take Frank along. He'd accepted the
offer of a ride to the Shannon Airport nonverbally, by throwing
his oversize duffle into the Ford's trunk and slamming its lid.

Danny was driving and Kerry was guiding them, using, as
Frank had foretold, more of Mrs. Musgrove's little message
slips. In any event, they barely needed them, as signs for the
round tower sprang up almost as soon as they'd left the hotel's
narrow lot. Shortly afterward, the tower itself appeared in the
distance: a little sunlit stone shaft—for the sun was out again—
rising above blue-gray hills. It grew majestically as they approached, acquiring a fringe of roofless buildings at its base. It
also acquired an eye. That is to say, two windows just below the
tower's conical roof came into perfect alignment with the road
they were following, allowing a glimpse straight through to the
blue sky beyond. In Danny's imagination, the tower became a
lighthouse, a beacon. Then the road turned, and the eye was
just another black hole in the stone.

"It must have been an abbey," Kerry was saying as he tried to find the place in his guidebook. Failing at that, he improvised. "St. Consonants. Founded before the Vikings came and rebuilt every year afterward. Sacked by Henry VIII's men in fifteen something or other. Or Elizabeth's or Cromwell's."

"The local people must still use it," Danny replied. "The grounds, I mean."

Between their road and the tower was a cemetery, dotted with Celtic crosses. Many of the stones looked new, and a few had flowers set out before them.

"Slow down," Kerry said. "There's the drive already."

Danny turned left in front of an oncoming farm tractor pulling a wagon twice its size, saying, "We're late," by way of her excuse.

The lane was narrow for the big sedan and winding. Ahead of them, Danny could see a rambling farmhouse of the same brown stone as the ruined abbey.

Maybe it's the very same stone, she thought, remembering Frank's earlier remark about scavenging masons. She would have asked him—he was standing amongst chickens in a dirt courtyard before the house—if his first words to them hadn't wiped the subject from her mind.

"He's on his way here now," Frank said, bending to look through her open window. "Harty Doan."

"He knows you're leaving?"

"I don't know. It doesn't matter. You'd better get away while you can."

"Get in," Kerry said, "and we'll all get away."

Frank hesitated, retrieved a knapsack from the farmhouse steps, and froze again. "Too late," he said.

Danny, who'd climbed out of the car to give him the driver's seat, looked back across the abbey's graveyard. A black van was speeding toward them down the Killaloe road.

"Is there another way out of here?" she asked.

"There is," he said, tossing her the knapsack and racing for the house. "Get in!"

Danny ran around the car, colliding with Kerry, who was looking down the road in the wrong direction. She bundled him and the knapsack into the backseat beside Max and climbed into the front. By then, Frank was back. He handed her a length of stout chain and a stouter padlock.

As they shot away, Max broke his silence. "How much do you owe him? Maybe we can just pay it."

"Millions for defense but not one penny for tribute!" Kerry cried.

Frank followed a rutted track that circled the house. The ruts were mere traces on that portion of the track that wove through outbuildings old and new, but they grew so deep on the open hillside beyond that the heavily laden Ford bottomed out repeatedly.

Presently they arrived at a modern steel gate set in a well-maintained stone wall.

Frank made to get out, but Danny stopped him. "I'll do it."

She opened the gate for them and the Ford squeezed through. Above them on the hill, the black van appeared around the corner of the house, careening crazily.

"Two turns through the ring in the post and around the gate," Frank called from his open window.

Danny made the two loops with the heavy chain, not daring to look at the van but hearing its springs groan as it rocked down the hill. She fumbled with the lock, nearly closing it before she had the shackle through the chain's ends. Then she felt someone come up behind her and reach around her like a dance partner.

"Easy now," Frank crooned. "Plenty of time."

His big hands took the padlock from hers and snapped it home.

"Now run for your life."

Kerry was half out his door's open window, and Danny gave him a push as she ran past. She turned at her own door in time to see a burly man without a hair on his pink head shaking his fist at them from beyond the locked gate. Kerry was shaking his own fist in defiant reply.

He was still shaking it as they sped away and he settled into his seat. "The old clichés are the best," he said happily.

CHAPTER TEN

"Part Two is the land of doubt."
—*Camelot Guide to Romance Writing*

In short order, they went from unpaved lanes to country roads and then to the N18, the highway that would take them north to Galway. Kerry was already rehearsing the story of their escape for future tellings, and doing it with so much joy that even Max, who had sat through the real thing with folded arms, began to smile. Danny mistook that smile, as she had so many of Max's in years past. She decided it meant that they would part friends at the Shannon Airport, with no hard feelings between them.

But they didn't part, didn't even leave the highway for the airport.

"I'm sticking with you," Max said when the first exit sign was sighted. "Now that I've seen what you're into over here, I'm afraid to leave you. What if this Doan guy tracks you down?"

So the airport exit came and went, and the four fell into the routine of traveling. Frank was intent on his driving and Kerry on his guidebook, held flat on his knees. Max fell asleep. From her place in the navigator's seat, Danny studied the glories of County Clare's long central valley, its rolling farmland and the autumn gold beyond the hedgerows. This study gave her the chance to watch her side mirror for a glimpse of the black van. Almost as important, it enabled her to avoid watching the oncoming traffic. Frank's driving, though precise, was very fast.

Danny's right foot pressed repeatedly on a phantom brake pedal that would have been a real one in any civilized car. And it was only with a great effort that she kept herself from reaching for an equally imaginary steering wheel whenever Frank made one of his swooping passes.

Around Crusheen they passed through a brief shower. On its far side, Kerry shut his book, the better to tap the back of Danny's head with it.

"You've got to look at this guidebook, Sis. There's a whole section on *The Quiet Man* and where they filmed it."

From behind the wheel, Frank said, "That again," a warning neither Furey heeded.

"What I'm thinking is, why not hit a few of these on our way through Connemara? I'd like to see them, and it would be great research for our book."

"What book would that be?" Frank asked.

"*The Fureys' Complete Quiet Man,* or whatever we decide to call it. Danny and I were thinking of writing it when we were over here the last time."

"And now you're thinking of it again?"

"*He's* thinking," Danny said.

"What?" Kerry demanded. "You're backing out so soon?"

Danny made a show of studying the scenery again. "I think we should stick to the original plan," she said. "Just for a change of pace. Let's find Letterfenny and then see how you're feeling. If you want to tackle more, we can talk about it."

"I'll be talking," Kerry said. "You'll be packing. Are you saying you'd pass up a trip to these places? White o' Morn and Cohan's? And don't tell me you'll come over later and do it. I don't want you cutting me out of this."

"What now?" asked Max, awakened from his nap.

"Seriously, Danny. This is important for you, too. You could have a book reach a second printing. *That* would be a change of pace."

"Thanks for thinking of me."

"You're welcome. What do you say, Frank? Does it sound like fun?"

"As much fun as a tour of famous English depredations," the Irishman replied. He was leaning forward in his seat, suddenly, as though peering through a mist. "Or visiting famine sites. Would there be a list of those in your book?"

The remark drew Danny's attention from the scenery, though she regretted turning her head immediately, as they were passing a Land Rover that was itself passing an ancient Citroen, so that they were temporarily three abreast on the two-lane road.

"What does *The Quiet Man* have to do with depredations and famine?" Kerry asked.

Frank shrugged. "It's another blot on this blotted country. That similarity enough?"

"Not to mention being a waste of good film stock," Max contributed.

"Look at that field," Danny said. "Is that wheat or hay?"

"I take it you feel the way I do about that epic," Max said to the back of Frank's head.

"I do. I'd never heard much good of it or bothered myself to sit through it until I moved to Boston. Then it was all I could do to avoid it, especially the week of St. Patrick's Day. That's a crazy time there altogether. Did you know the drunks march in the streets in Boston on the feast itself?"

"I've heard that," Kerry said.

"Finally I sat down and watched the damn thing. At the end of a long St. Paddy's Day shift behind a bar. It was being shown on a channel that called itself the 'superstation.' How American is that? I was dead tired, but so many people had asked me if I'd seen *The Quiet Man* that day or praised it to the heavens, I decided I had to know what they were talking about. So I poured myself a Bushmills and settled in. Let me tell you, the next drunk who mentioned *The Quiet Man* to me was deaf for a week."

Danny started to say something when Frank, downshifting from fourth to first as they rounded a bend, shook the thought from her head.

The driver's own thoughts were unaffected. "I knew the story, of course. American boxer comes back to Ireland to buy the farm where he was born. But what an Ireland he came back to. What a collection of cardboard and tinsel. And so dated and so stereotyped. My secondhand telly was in danger of flying out the window the whole time I was watching the slander."

"It was released in 1952," Danny said.

"Even then it must have insulted every man, woman, and child living over here. The women especially. That's the worst of it: its view of women. Dowry slaves without as much spunk as the sheep they tend barefoot. Barefoot! Who would ever walk behind a flock of sheep in bare feet?"

"Mary Kate Danaher," Kerry supplied.

"Right. But then, she was a woman who actually wanted to be dragged along the ground in front of the whole county so everyone would know how much her brand-new American husband loved her. I suppose if she'd had a tooth knocked out, she would have had it mounted."

"It was her brother lost the tooth," Kerry said, but not loud enough to actually interrupt.

"That's the business that really tore it for me. The scene where John Wayne saddles up his horse and rides off to the train station to find his bolted wife like he's going after a stray heifer in *Red River.* I was surprised he didn't rope the missus when he found her. It wouldn't have been any worse than dragging her along by the scruff of her neck, while the colorful townsfolk are cheering him on. And arming him, God save us. 'Here's a stick to beat the lovely lady.' If he'd so much as waved that stick at a real Irishwoman, he'd have ended with it stuck so far up his ass he'd have gotten splinters in his toothbrush every morning."

Max laughed at this, and it was something more than the salesman's chuckle that Danny always imagined him using for customers' jokes.

He said, "You should have heard my sister Kay, the feminist, go off after Danny just clicked by *The Quiet Man* one St. Patrick's Day. Kay couldn't understand how any woman could like that movie, never mind love it."

Danny thought of trotting out the arguments she'd used with Kay that day. The film was a historical document, not a picture of contemporary Ireland or even Ireland of the fifties. It was based on a short story written in the thirties and set in the twenties. John Ford, the director, hadn't done enough to establish the period, only suggesting it in vague ways, like his references to the Irish Civil War and elements of stage dressing like the movie's single ancient automobile.

That line of reasoning had done her so little good with Kay that she didn't bother to air it out now. She twisted in her seat instead, intending to ask her brother if he was enjoying the trip. But Kerry's long nose was once again burrowed in his book.

CHAPTER ELEVEN

"Can your heroine's favorite color be a key to her character?
How about her favorite movie?"
—*Camelot Guide to Romance Writing*

They arrived in Galway in time for tea or a Guinness, Max and
Kerry voting for the latter option. Frank spent most of the
stop—at a pub just off the town's park-like central square—on
the phone with local friends.

"Getting a recommendation for a place to stop for the night,"
he explained when they'd started out again, this time traveling
west on the N59. "Oughterard's the very place. Nice little town
with restaurants and pubs and a hotel that caters to Americans.
Only it's full. But there's a little fishing lodge right on the lake.
On Lough Corrib, that is. Clean rooms and a good breakfast
every morning. And the beds have electric heaters."

Danny asked, "You've stayed at this lodge?"

"No. But my friends have. Liddle's, it's called. I phoned
ahead. They're holding rooms for us for as many nights as we
want them."

"Nights?" Max asked, taking the word from Danny's mouth.

"Sure. These two want to make a tour of movie locations,
don't they? Or is pilgrimage the word I want? Oughterard is the
perfect base for either."

"I didn't think you were interested in that idea," Danny said.

"I'm not. But I'm just the hired help."

Kerry leaned forward and patted his sister's shoulder. Then, his emotion unspent, he repeated the action on Frank's. "This will be great. As long as the place doesn't smell of fish."

"The whole trip does," Danny said, producing laughter from her sibling that she declined to join.

Liddle's was a modern lodge, by Irish standards, built in the sixties, flat-roofed and unprepossessing from its gravel car park but spacious and inviting within. The walls of the entry were hung with framed collections of brilliantly colored flies, each one tied by Cam Liddle, the owner, and available for purchase. The lounge, where a peat fire burned and where the new arrivals found Mrs. Liddle, pink and smiling, was furnished in large pieces covered in dull leather or coarse fabric, chairs and sofas that weary fishermen could settle into wet and happy. Fishermen or dogs. Two black Labradors were keeping Mrs. Liddle company. The younger rose with her to greet her guests. The older, fatter one maintained its watch on the smoky blaze.

Kerry did the registering for all of them: one room for the men and another for Danny.

Mrs. Liddle didn't question the sleeping arrangements, asking only, "Will any of you be fishing then? My husband's available to take you out tomorrow."

"I might try my hand," said Max, who hadn't gotten farther into the place than the exhibit of flies. He said it almost as a question, and that directed to Kerry.

"Go for it," Kerry replied.

Danny was still wondering at that exchange as she unpacked in her room, wondering too at the odds of the place recommended by Frank's unnamed Galway friends being one that catered to Max's principal weakness.

Once unpacked, she tried to decide which of her four narrow beds she would use. All the lodge's rooms had four, being intended for parties of sportsmen. Danny lay down on one merely to test it, thinking of Goldilocks and even phrasing a joke comparing herself to that famous housebreaker. She was playing variations on the theme when she dropped off to sleep.

She was awakened by a knocking on her door. The lake visible through the window beyond her still-shod feet was dull silver with the last of the daylight. She checked her watch and found that it was almost nine.

The knock sounded again. Danny rose and opened the door, anxious for a private word with Kerry. She found Frank instead, red hair brushed and face aglow, dressed in jeans and a heavy black sweater that covered him to his chin.

"I thought all our driving might have worn you out," he said with a nod. "The brother and I are going into town for dinner. Are you interested?"

Azure blue, Danny thought, suddenly hitting on the very word to describe the color of Frank's eyes. She'd looked azure up once, after years of using it carelessly, and learned that it meant the blue of a clear sky. But what sky? she'd then asked. What time of day? Of year? And seen from where? All those quibbles were forgotten as she stared into these two eyes and pronounced them azure blue.

What a blessing, she thought, *in this land of rains and overcasts, to have men roaming about whose eyes are the promise of a perfect day.*

"What about Max?" she asked.

"He's tying flies with Cam Liddle. He may be Max's true love."

"I knew it wasn't me. Give me fifteen minutes," she added and hurried off to figure out the shower.

They had their dinner in the Oughterard Hotel, the modern, almost American place that had been too full to offer them rooms. Danny expected a strong and negative reaction from Kerry to its well-lit dining room and to its menu, which included "chicken fingers," but he settled in happily enough at their corner table. He'd left his poteen in his room and so made do with a stout, as did his companions, Frank drinking deeply of his after his long afternoon at the wheel.

After neglecting his meal, a small salad, for the time it took Frank and Danny to wolf down theirs, Kerry roused himself and looked about him.

"Americans everywhere. And cameras, too. They probably sleep with them." Then he snapped his fingers. "We'll need a camera. We've got to photograph every *Quiet Man* site we visit. It'd cost us a fortune to have someone else do it later."

Frank sighed into his stout.

Danny said, "I have a camera you're welcome to use. You can have the photo credit."

"Not enough glory in that," her brother replied. He straightened himself in his chair and handed his salad bowl to a passing waitress. "My contribution will be more substantive. For example, I think I've figured out who the Mystery Man is."

He was seated next to Frank, and now he leaned toward him, conspiratorially. "We're about to discuss *The Quiet Man* in earnest. You might want to step out for a smoke."

"Do your worst. I'll need to develop some calluses if I'm to make it through this trip."

"Ear calluses," Danny said.

"So what's this about a mystery man?"

"*The* Mystery Man," Kerry insisted. "Well, when you watch a movie about a hundred times, the way Danny and I have watched *The Quiet Man*, you stop seeing the action in the center of the screen and start noticing the corners. Or the background, to speak three dimensionally. That's how we came to spot the Mystery Man in the first place. He's this unidentified guy who hangs around the Widow Turlane, Mildred Natwick's character. She's the old aristocrat Victor McLaglen has the hots for."

"Is sweet on," Frank corrected. "Those two couldn't even get warm."

"You first see the Mystery Man in the scene where John Wayne tries to buy his boyhood cottage from the widow. The old guy is leaning on the fireplace mantel in the widow's parlor, watching everything. Danny thinks he's just some unnamed relative of Natwick's or maybe her butler."

"I never said butler," Danny muttered.

"But the other night, when I was watching the thing in the wee small hours, the truth was revealed to me. It's her dead husband. Think about it. He's old and well dressed. He's always standing in the corner of the shot. Nobody ever looks at him, nobody ever addresses him. The only time he really does anything is when Natwick catches Maureen O'Hara's bouquet at the start of the courting business. Then he looks from Natwick to McLaglen, the first husband looking at the next one.

"And he gets a bow at the end. Why would an actor with no lines and nothing to do get a bow?"

"A bow?" Frank asked.

Danny answered him. "Ford gave the principal actors a curtain call at the end of the movie. The ones who were on location anyway. The ones who only appear in the studio shots, like Sean McClory and Ken Curtis, didn't get one. You don't remember that part?"

"Must have been after I threw my shoe at the television."

"The point is," Kerry said, "the ghost gets a bow. And that's not all. I said before that none of the other actors ever looks at him, but that's not true. The one who shares his bow, the actor who plays McLaglen's flunky, Feeny—"

"Jack MacGowran," Danny said.

"Right. During their little two-second good-bye shot, MacGowran doesn't just look at the camera like everyone else does. He smiles and looks at the ghost, like he's letting us in on an inside joke."

"Maybe the old man is someone Ford thought the audience would recognize," Danny countered. "Irish audiences anyway. Maybe it's Maurice Walsh, who wrote the story, or some old star from the Abbey Players."

"Nope," Kerry said, smiling up beatifically at the woman who had come to deliver their check. "It's a ghost."

"If it is," Frank said, "it's the only true Irish touch in the movie."

"You believe in ghosts?" Danny asked.

"Of course. It's only another way of saying that I believe in the past. And more, that I believe the past can reach forward and seize the present by the throat.

"Now drink up. It's been a busy day."

Chapter Twelve

*"Your heroine's subconscious desires
must undercut her conscious ones."*
—*Camelot Guide to Romance Writing*

The three were on the road in good time the next morning, but not so early as Max and Cam Liddle had set out. The morning was made for fishing or anything out-of-doors: a deep blue sky set off by ragged bits of cloud, a breeze just shy of a wind, and everywhere the rich pure light of autumn. Oughterard styled itself "the Gateway to Connemara," and certainly the landscape began to change before they'd left the village far behind. The houses thinned out, as did the trees. As did the green in general. Then mountains, appearing in the distance—barren giants— miniaturized everything before them.

Their first stop was "The Quiet Man Bridge." Kerry spotted its modest sign, having been forewarned of it by his guidebook. The bridge itself was also modest, its stone covered by lichen as thick as a light snow, its single stone arch crossing a stream that the road had been following for some time, connecting the road with a farm or two beyond. But simple or not, it delighted Kerry, and his delight was contagious.

"John Wayne and Barry Fitzgerald stopped here in their little cart. Wayne got his first glimpse of 'White o' Morn' from this very spot." They'd left their car by the roadside and crossed the bridge on foot. "Those mountains there are the very ones you see in the background. But where's the cottage? Don't tell me they tore it down."

"Not necessarily," Danny said. "They could have used a cottage somewhere else and edited the shots together so it looked like it was here. They do it all the time in the movies."

Frank said, "Get together, you two. I'll take your author photo. You needn't give me a credit."

She and Kerry took a dozen additional shots between them, and then they set out again. North to Maam with mountains on either side of the road now, lean tawny mountains like the haunches of lions, the cloud shadows passing across them faster than the car on its road. At Maam they turned east, having gained the northern shore of Lough Corrib at last. Immediately the countryside began to soften. The lake came into view and disappeared again a dozen times as they drove. Sometimes an island could be seen, sometimes two or three, and, once, an island with a ruined tower. They were in sight of it when Kerry ordered Danny to stop.

He was out of the car a second later, following a path through a fuchsia hedge as tall as a man. Beyond it was a bright green plot, beyond that a tufted brown field, and beyond both of those the lake and the little island with the tumbled turret, looking like the conning tower of a medieval submarine.

"Recognize it?" Kerry asked when the others had caught him up. Frank said no and Danny, photographing away, said nothing.

"The scene where John Wayne is walking back from Castletown after O'Hara strands him there? He's boiling mad and kicks a rock about a mile? That island is in the background. He has to have walked right along here."

Danny was unconvinced, and they stood disputing the point like rival theologians until Frank, in protest, marched back to the car, crushed fuchsia blooms a blood trail in his wake. The

Fureys, chastened, hurried after him.

But Kerry could not contain his excitement for long. Not even when they caught their first sight of Cong and found it to be nothing like a Technicolor movie. To Danny at least, the place was small and dark, the latter impression created by a general lack of fresh paint and a gathering overcast. There was no one about to ask directions of, but they didn't need them, not with Kerry on the job.

"There's Cohan's! Cohan's Pub! Pull over, Frank. Park anywhere."

It was the movie pub—it had a sign to prove it—but not a real pub. Kerry, forewarned by his guidebook that the building contained a dry goods store, was not too disappointed, only glowering very slightly at the gas pumps that now stood where Barry Fitzgerald's horse had once parked itself from long habit.

Danny was standing in the center of the road, in a wide spot—the locals might have called it a square—created when the road split in two to pass around a stone monument. The monument was not much bigger in footprint than one of the gas pumps, though taller, and might have been an unambitious cross. Certainly it had a cross member, but one very near the top and so small in relationship to the stone's height that it resembled the brim of a hat set on an Easter Island head.

No plaque identified the artifact, and Danny couldn't decipher its worn lettering. She wasn't interested in its origins in any case, only in whether it had been photographed by a certain cinematographer in 1951.

"Recognize this, Kerry?"

The expert, coming over at a trot, did recognize it. He ran a hand over it lovingly. "Of course. It's in the long shot of the pub. When Wayne and O'Hara come down the hill on the bicycle built for two."

He turned to explain the reference to Frank, but the Irish

film critic was up with him and more. "After they escape from their chaperone during the courting nonsense." He was trying to sound dismissive, even severe, but failing in the face of the Americans' great happiness.

"Right," Kerry said. "That means they rode down this way." He trotted off again. "They made the turn at full speed, O'Hara screaming her head off."

"They never could have made that turn," Danny said, surveying it. "The road's too narrow at the T."

"We know they made it, Sis. It's in the movie."

"The Bible," Frank corrected.

"Then the road must have been changed sometime in the past fifty years," Danny said. "Maybe they narrowed it when they built that house across the street."

"That house? There? That's been there since the Normans came."

The siblings stood arguing about it until Kerry, looking down the T road, spotted the stretch over which the Reverend Mr. Playfair had driven his bishop in the film's last scene, with the whole village turned out and cheering "like Protestants." They moved from there to the vicar's very house, from which Wayne and O'Hara had borrowed the hallowed bicycle. The little stone cottage was now covered with ivy to a remarkable degree, walls and roof, dark green ivy shot through with streaks of red.

The play of colors made the place for Kerry, reminding him of an exchange between Playfair and his good wife. He threw the first line down gauntlet-like before his sister: " 'Only an American would think of emerald green.' "

" 'Red's more durable,' " Danny replied, but sotto voce, so as not to provoke their driver.

Beyond the cottage was a stream. A trout stream, Kerry declared, hurrying along it in search of the spot where Ward Bond, playing the parish priest, had hooked and lost his record fish. Danny and Frank followed more slowly, admiring the brook itself.

"I've been thinking that your brother came over to visit his past," Frank said. "Not Ireland. Do you know what I'm saying? The trip from ten years ago and that night in the pub when he got roaring drunk, that has such a strange hold on him. It's almost like he couldn't find his photo album of your last trip, so he flew across to visit his snaps in person. Now it seems more like he came to visit a movie. Very Disneyland."

"We came to find our grandfather's village," Danny reminded him, though that was fast becoming more a statement of faith than of fact. "Our father always wanted to do it, but never got the chance."

"And you say you don't believe in ghosts."

They came to the ruins of an abbey, set between the brook and the town. Unlike the one that abutted the house of Frank's aunt, this abbey was being maintained. That is, the grounds were being maintained; the buildings were only flint-colored fragments. Frank and Danny walked the monks' columned cloister, which framed a flat green lawn. Danny was distracted by a glimpse of a figure in brown hurrying away from them along the far side of the colonnade, appearing and disappearing as it passed each of the little archways, the visitor's drab color of dress making Danny wonder if one of the ancient monks had returned. This distraction lasted a moment only, she was that conscious of the man beside her. So conscious of him in fact that she failed to raise her guard when he broached the subject of her books.

"I'm reading your *Beyond Forever*. It's very . . . romantic."

"They're not called romance novels because they're written in a Romance language. Kerry give you that?"

"Yes, last night, when we were turning in. Your heroine, Beverly, is not at all like yourself."

Danny laughed. "Why type short and dark when it's just as easy to type blonde and tall? My readers want to pass through the looking glass, not stare into one. Escape, you know?"

"And their author? Kerry said you didn't start writing these things until after your divorce. Were they part of your escape?"

There was much for Danny not to like in the question, beginning with the dismissal of her books as "these things." But she answered mildly enough. "I needed the money. Max had expensive tastes. I was on the hook for a lot of the Pouilly-Fuissé he'd pissed away."

"He still has those tastes," Frank said. "Did you know that your brother is paying Max's way over here?"

"I suspected it," she said, remembering Max's question about the fishing.

"But I wasn't thinking of money when I asked if the books were your escape hatch. I was thinking of the romance angle."

Danny was ahead of him—or thought she was. "You think I fell into writing books in which love conquers all because love hadn't come through for me and I needed my faith restored?"

"No. I'm wondering if you write books that make a mockery of romance, by making it a formula and a cliché, because you've turned your back on your faith."

Danny was distracted from this indictment by the brush of Frank's hand against hers. Her reaction was an effective reply to the charge he'd just made against her, although she didn't recognize it for that. He—deep in thought—seemed unaware of the contact. Nor, when he'd roused himself, did he acknowledge it, saying instead, "Where's that brother of yours gotten off to now?"

Kerry was nowhere about the abbey, nowhere along the stream. They walked back into the village, scanning the shops they passed for him, Frank earnestly and Danny less so.

Kerry then appeared at the head of the street, supporting a

bicycle that was old enough to need supporting.

Now what? Danny asked herself.

The wanderer stood at the top of the hill and let Frank and Danny come to him. The pair found themselves above the little square where their car was parked, Cohan's Pub and the stone monument just below.

"I couldn't find a two-seater," Kerry said. "Nobody in town owns one. You'd think they'd keep one around for the tourists. The lady who runs the tea shop lent me this. I promised her we'd be back for a cuppa afterward, whatever that is."

"After what now?" Frank asked.

"After we prove to this naysayer, my sister, that Wayne and O'Hara could have made that turn at the bottom of the hill, narrow street or no narrow street. Danny will sit on the seat and hold her legs out. You'll stand on the pedals. You won't need to do much pedaling once you're going. Braking will be the thing."

Frank looked from him to the bicycle, dubious and then more dubious. "Does it have brakes, then?"

Kerry worked hand levers connected by rods to calipers that squeaked in response. Whether that squeak was a yes or a no to Frank's question, none of the three could say.

The barman turned driver hesitated, but only for a moment. "Right, we'll do it. Confusion to our enemies."

"What do you mean 'we'?" Danny asked. And to her brother: "*You* sit on the seat."

"That wouldn't be scientific. It's gotta be a woman. It's a center of gravity thing. Give me your camera. I'll run down to the corner and record everything for posterity, if there is any."

"Stop the cross traffic instead," Frank said, "if there is any."

Before Danny could object again, her brother was halfway down the hill and Frank was straddling the bike. "No escape hatch this time," he said.

She climbed up behind him, wording a remark about a "booby hatch" that she never got to use. They shot away more quickly than she'd expected, wobbling dangerously at first, the conveyance making a wheezing sound as a tire rubbed its fender. As they gained speed, Frank steered a straighter line, crouching over the handlebars. Danny's grim face was to one side of Frank's shoulder, her short legs stretched out left and right like wings.

Below them, she saw Kerry smiling with joy and forgetting the camera entirely. As the bicycle entered the curve, Danny provided the missing touch and the perfect one: Maureen O'Hara's scream.

CHAPTER THIRTEEN

"Never resolve one conflict before you've introduced another."
—Camelot Guide to Romance Writing

The ride back from Cong was so long that even Kerry had tired of reliving the day by the time they reached Oughterard. Luckily, once home, the three found they had no immediate need to speak. At dinner, in a place whose Gaelic name had more letters than its dining room had tables, a sunburned Max regaled them with his day on the lake with Cam Liddle. Only the guide's catch-and-release policy had kept Max from providing dinner for all, and breakfast, too.

When Max wearied of describing his many casts, Danny attempted to broach the subject of Letterfenny, using the steamed mussels they were eating as her segue. According to the menu, the shellfish were from Killary Harbor, the long finger of the sea that drained all the land around Leenane, the land, Danny pointed out, on which their grandfather's ghost town surely stood. The notion spoiled Kerry's slight appetite without engaging his interest, which was all caught up in a new plan that he announced with the arrival of dessert: They should scour the pubs of Oughterard in search of *Quiet Man* eyewitnesses.

"You should have done that back in Cong," said Frank, who was philosophically contemplating his black, untouched coffee.

"We'll start here and radiate outward."

"Drink your way across Connemara, you mean?"

80

Kerry, who had been steadily refilling his water glass from his poteen bottle, could make no effective reply. In any case, Frank hadn't paused for one.

"Well, you won't be the first Americans to try that. Drop me at the lodge on your way."

"And me," said Max. "Cam wants me to try a trout stream tomorrow."

Danny ran the two back to the lodge, wishing that she were being dropped in their stead. Kerry was unsteady on his feet before they'd entered their first pub, the first of three, as it turned out. Danny ordered a glass of Smithwick's in the first place, the one farthest from Liddle's, and switched to ginger ale in the second and third. Her brother ordered whatever she did and then contrived to spill his drink or empty into Danny's glass when no one was looking. He then refilled his glass-of-the-moment from the bottle he carried in his blazer's groaning pocket.

Between these bouts of slyness, Kerry questioned anyone who would listen regarding *The Quiet Man.* Danny stood by him, more as a guardian of public order than a participant, as she was embarrassed both by her brother's blunt technique and by his lack of success. From the start they encountered two difficulties: finding anyone old enough to remember the events of 1951 and getting those few they found to take Kerry's questioning seriously. Some professed not to know the film. Others shared Frank's low opinion of it. A few even managed to squeeze in below that very low bar. Luckily, those few spoke their scorn so rapidly and with so much Irish in their speech—and West Irish too—that the Fureys barely understood them and their tenderer feelings were spared.

The third pub, Doolin's, was just down the road from the fishing lodge. In it, a dank, smoky place where they appeared to be the only tourists, the Fureys received the standard shrugs and mumbled derision. Danny was introducing the subject of bed, jingling her car keys to hold Kerry's attention, when someone tapped her shoulder.

She turned and found a man only slightly taller than herself and very much older. Movie besotted as she was, Danny often classified people in terms of the actors they resembled. The stranger lacked a moustache, but he nevertheless reminded Danny of an elderly Douglas Fairbanks Jr.: white-haired, dignified, and wrinkled, though this specimen was more weathered than even that sun-damaged movie star. He was a Fairbanks who had been left out in the wind and rain, who hadn't shaved that day and perhaps not the day before, and who dressed eccentrically, in the jacket of a banker's suit over a zipped sweater, over a white shirt, frayed and grayed.

Then Danny's roving gaze was caught and held by the man's eyes, as blue-gray as the Irish stone and as ageless. "My name is Conneely," he said. "Donal Conneely. That's Donal, not Donald. One D, if you please. No O on the tail end, either, should you be inclined toward the Latino, as I hear you Yanks are these days."

When Danny hesitated, Kerry supplied the Furey end of the introduction. The old man nodded when he heard their family name and smiled to himself.

"You'll forgive my eavesdropping," he began, speaking slowly and distinctly. "I couldn't help overhearing your asking about *The Quiet Man.*"

"Do you remember the filming?" Kerry asked.

"Me? No. I was in another part of the country entirely. But I know many who remember that time—fifty years ago and more—and bless it, too."

He paused and cleared his throat, his very dry throat. Danny noticed that, alone among the patrons of the pub, Conneely carried no glass. Kerry noticed, too, and asked their new acquaintance if he'd join them for a pint.

The old man contemplated the offer for some time, even consulting the pub's wall clock, though that very noncommittal instrument was missing its hands. "I will then," he said.

Kerry announced a trip to the facilities, so Danny ordered the round—from a young man in a bright red vest worn over a T-shirt—and fetched it back. As Kerry had not returned, Danny and Conneely stood eyeing one another. Danny thought she had the measure of the man, but she was disconcerted to see that the other's flinty gaze conveyed the very same certainty regarding her.

To deflect that gaze, Danny said, "We haven't met many people over here who bless *The Quiet Man*."

"Nor will you," Conneely replied, "among folk like these, your farmers and fishermen and mechanics. You have to speak to people whose bread is buttered by you tourists. Shopkeepers, restaurant owners. And tour guides, like myself. We know that movie's brought more Americans to Ireland than Aer Lingus."

Only when Kerry returned did Conneely raise the pint Danny had handed him. His "to your very good health" came out with a long gap between the third and fourth words, the break caused by the sight of Kerry refilling his own glass without taking the poteen bottle from his pocket.

"I was just telling your sister that I'm a tour guide. I've many specialties, and one is *The Quiet Man*. Sign up with me by the day or by the week, and I'll take you to every location they used and stand you where the camera stood itself. If you can't see John Wayne and Maureen O'Hara as plain as this pint, it's the fault of your own imaginations and nothing else. In between stops, I'll tell you stories about the production known only to God and myself."

"You reserved him for the week, I hope," Kerry said, addressing Danny.

"It's the first time I've heard the offer." Danny tried to retain her brother's attention, but Kerry was already getting down to particulars.

"Can you put us in touch with people who remember the shooting?"

"Certainly I can. With the locals they used as extras, those that are still alive, and with others who simply looked on in awe and wonder."

"How about White o' Morn, John Wayne's cottage? We didn't find it near The Quiet Man Bridge."

"No man could. It's miles away, near Maam. But it's just an old ruin that the winds howl through, as the poet says. Not many know the way to it, but I can take you there."

"Speaking of ruins," Danny said, shouldering her way into the conversation, "do you know a ghost town near Leenane called Letterfenny?"

"Ghost town? Sounds like something out of a western. You Yanks have an intriguing language, but sometimes it's less than precise. Every town is a ghost town, when you stop and think about it. Full of dead people, dead hopes, and dead dreams."

"Letterfenny," Danny repeated. "Have you ever heard of it?"

"I have not. But what do you say to my proposition? Will I make this the most memorable trip of your young lives or no?"

Danny spoke quickly, before Kerry could shake on the deal. "We've got a guidebook that's pretty comprehensive. I think we're doing okay on our own."

"Okay? Pretty comprehensive? You think? Tell me now, other than the immortal bridge, what exactly have you found?"

Kerry described their trip to Cong, finding an ally in Conneely in his ongoing debate with Danny regarding the disputed lakeside location they'd passed on the way. The old man nodded once for each find inside the village and clasped Kerry on the arm when the American described the run through the square on the tea shop's bicycle, the description taking far longer than the plunge itself.

"I wish I'd been there to see it. And what did you think of Ashford Castle?"

"Ashford Castle?" Danny asked, but of Kerry.

"Certainly Ashford Castle," Conneely replied. "The big luxury hotel on the lake. Didn't the stars of the movie all stay there, living like raja? And didn't they shoot half the movie on the castle grounds? You were only a mile from the place when you were in Cong. Didn't your comprehensive guidebook tell you that?"

"It's in there," Kerry said. "I guess I just didn't connect it with Cong. We can drive over in the morning."

"The hell we can," Danny said. "I'm not driving around that lake again."

"There, there," Conneely said. "Don't get your blood up. No harm's been done. I can get you there tomorrow and you won't have to drive a mile. No, nor see a foot of the road you saw today. I can arrange to take you across the lake by launch, a grand trip. We can tour the castle grounds, have a picnic lunch, and skip back across here in time for your tea. All for a very reasonable price."

"How reasonable?" Danny asked.

"Let me worry about that," Kerry said. "We've got to do this. I'm sure Mr. Conneely and I can make the numbers work."

"Donal, if you please."

"Thanks. Donal and I will discuss the details. You're bushed from the drive. Go to bed. I can walk back from here."

"That's right," Conneely said. "Go on now. But beware of the Irish ghosts and spirits on the road. Your headless women, fire-breathing hounds, whistling seals, and hares of any description. And don't fret about your brother. I won't keep him up too long. We'll all need our sleep if we're to get an early start."

CHAPTER FOURTEEN

"Happy times don't make happy books. Shovel on the woe."
—*Camelot Guide to Romance Writing*

Danny was reluctant to leave Kerry behind in the pub, feeling the ache of old disasters as an athlete feels old injuries and a soldier old wounds. She was reluctant but tempted, too, being very tired. And it was a very short walk back to the lodge. Not even Kerry, she was sure, could lose his way.

In the end she decided to go, but she also decided on a precaution. As she said goodnight to Conneely, Danny reached around her brother's blind side and extracted the bottle of poteen from its hiding place.

"Have your nightcap at home," she said.

Kerry barely shrugged in reply, excited as he was with this new project. He and Conneely had found a table and were bent over it like conspirators by the time Danny reached the pub's door.

Outside the night was soft and starlit. Danny paused to gaze up at those stars and to drink in a breeze that carried a hint of the lake. She weighed walking home herself, this during her struggle to find the unlocking button on Ford's key fob, but Conneely's inventory of ghosts was fresh in her mind. She told herself that she'd keep the car in second gear, limiting the harm that could come to her or it. On the rock-walled lane that led down from the main road to Liddle's, she never left first gear, the car slowing with a jerk whenever she lifted her foot from the gas pedal. Even so, the curving walls seemed to rush by like those of a luge run.

When she was halfway down that run, something streaked across the drive before her. "A hare of any description," Danny said to herself, braking the car to a halt to collect her wits. Immediately she felt again the sensation of being watched. She studied the road ahead and behind and saw nothing. Her view to either side was blocked by the border walls. Presumably these same walls blocked anyone else's view of her, but still the feeling of being someone's study persisted.

Leaving the headlights on and the engine running, Danny climbed out of the car to look around. To her left was the black descent to the lake. To her right, a little rise and on it a ruined cottage. There was a break in the roadside wall just where she stood. A former gateway to the former cottage perhaps. She stepped through the gap and climbed the little hill.

The cottage she found was rudely built, with walls fallen to waist height except where they were supported by the chimney and the rotting framework of the front door. Danny stood outside, looking over one wall, and saw that the floor plan was the same as that of John Wayne's movie cottage, White o' Morn: two rooms, one twice as large as the other, divided by an interior wall that contained the hearth.

She was thinking of the hard lives of the generations who had lived in that little place when the feeling of not being alone returned to her like a flush spreading over her skin. She looked up and saw the young woman of Limerick, standing on the far side of the far wall.

"Damn!" Danny said, starting so she nearly jumped.

The stranger was so close for once that Danny noticed first not the familiar coat or blue scarf but her eyes, large and frightened and black against the skin of a face so pale it seemed to glow in the starlight.

The thought that her own reaction had scared the watcher at least as much as the watcher had scared her calmed Danny somewhat. "Damn," she said again but softly. "You almost gave me a heart attack. Who are you? I mean, I've seen you before, haven't I? In Limerick?"

She remembered then the barely noted figure hurrying through the ruined cloister in Cong. "And this afternoon. Have you been following me?"

There was more sudden realization than tact in this last question, and it seemed to frighten the girl even more. She turned and fled into the darkness.

After a heartbeat's hesitation, Danny circled the cottage to follow her. But her hesitation and the detour had given her quarry all the lead she needed. When the American reached the far side of the hovel, she could see no sign of the young woman, no path down the weedy sloping ground.

CHAPTER FIFTEEN

*"The fear of repeating past mistakes should lead
directly to new mistakes."*
—*Camelot Guide to Romance Writing*

The front door of the lodge was locked, but Danny's room key opened it. She stepped into the entrance hall, now dark, and heard the sound of a man's voice coming from the lounge. An Irishman's voice, describing the challenge of fishing for trout at the bottom-most depths of the lake.

Danny meant to skirt the lounge as quietly as possible, but when she drew abreast of it, she saw Frank. He was sprawled in one of the leather chairs, wearing his heavy black sweater, the folds of its neck framing his face like an Amish beard. Danny had expected to see Max as well, but Frank was the lone audience for the fishing lecture, which was being delivered by a man Danny assumed to be the great Cam Liddle himself.

He was a bony-faced man with gnarled hands who wore tinted glasses though the room was lit only by the fire and a single lamp. He stopped in midsentence and turned in his chair when Frank spotted the lingering Danny.

"Did you lose himself, then?" Frank asked.

"He won't be long," Danny said, holding up her trophy bottle of poteen. "Sorry I interrupted."

"Not at all," Liddle said, rising to shake Danny's hand and formally welcome her to the lodge. "I was just off to walk Kelsey.

Come on, girl." The older, fatter of the two house Labradors padded out of the shadows and followed Liddle to the door.

Danny held the fisherman there with a question. "Do you have a young woman staying here? She wears a brown coat and a blue scarf."

Liddle chuckled. "I know my guests by their names, not their overcoats. The only young lady we have at present is yourself. Why do you ask?"

"I thought I saw someone I knew along your drive."

"Oh? Kelsey and I will scout around."

Danny waited until the front door had closed behind man and dog. Then she turned reluctantly to Frank.

"Who's this woman you thought you knew?" he asked. "A friend from the States?"

"Just someone I've been seeing on and off since I got here. I mentioned her to you at King John's Castle."

"That one? Way out here? Is that likely?" When he got no answer, Frank added, "Does she carry a book? Maybe she's wanting your autograph."

Danny laughed along with him at the idea. "Maybe. Goodnight, I guess."

"Guess again," Frank said, uncrossing and recrossing his long legs. "Take a seat and wait up with me. It'll be a miracle if that brother of yours has a key to let himself in with."

Danny entered the sunken lounge, a single step down from the hallway, and took the seat opposite Frank. Sat on its edge, tentatively. Then, swinging the bottle between her legs, she described their meeting with Donal Conneely, the freelance tour guide.

"Give me that before you break it," Frank said at length, holding his hand out for the poteen. "I wish you'd thought to get Kerry's wallet as well. Then we'd be sure he'd come back. He's probably buying rounds for the house right now."

Danny shrugged, the gesture meant to convey that her brother might as well spend his money as he liked before some hospital got it.

"But I'm just as glad we've this quiet moment," Frank was saying. "I want to ask you about your family."

"I haven't much," Danny said, drawing her knees together.

"You had a father and mother. Science teaches us that."

"Why do you want to know about them?"

"I'm trying to figure your brother out, I guess. He's a fascinating study."

Danny suspected that she herself was the subject of Frank's curiosity and not her brother. Then she wondered if that was a suspicion or an exercise in vanity. "Suppose you take the lead," she said, in part to stall, in part to satisfy her own curiosity. "What were your parents like?"

"Irish clichés, offensive ones, the pair of them, like your barefoot shepherdess. A man who drank and beat his wife and a woman who took it praying, until her son got old enough to put a stop to it."

"Then you took care of her until you decided to try America?"

"Until she passed on and I decided to try America. Your turn."

"What would you like to know?"

"Your father and Kerry. They were very close, I suppose."

"Like a man and his shadow. He was a happy guy, with a lot of friends, our father." *Who art in heaven,* her tired mind added all on its own.

"Did he die of leukemia?"

"No. Automobile accident."

"And your mom's down in Florida? Were you her shadow?"

"Her clone," Danny said.

"So she was small and dark and striking?" Frank asked, smiling as he often did to pull the rug from beneath his words.

"She was quiet," Danny said.

"That isn't much of a picture. I thought you were a word-smith."

"On descriptions I'm a believer in the apt detail. Camelot readers won't sit still for a laundry list."

"And Kerry was the one who took care of your mother after your dad passed?"

"There's a difference of opinion there. She might have taken care of him, until she got tired of New Jersey winters."

"You were out in Iowa?"

"Ohio."

"With Max?"

Here we are finally. "Yes. I thought holding my marriage together was my priority. It was a misplaced priority, as it turned out. Max wanted a reliable second income, not a wife." *Damn that Smithwick's,* she added to herself.

"And what were you looking for in him?"

"Free fish."

"Sounds like a match made in heaven," Frank said. "What happened?"

A friend of mine named Lola happened, Danny thought. *Happened into our bed.* She shrugged.

"He's a little young for his age is Max," Frank observed cautiously.

There was a time when Danny would have rushed through that half-open door. But she'd been divorced for years now and had had a further experience of men, so she merely shrugged and said, "It's the current style in American males. We— American females—have pronounced them unnecessary, and they've taken to it."

Frank reached for the room's only functioning lamp, a reading lamp made from a boat's binnacle light, saying, "I'm a fool to be mentioning your ex, when we've been given a quiet moment."

He switched off the light, leaving them with the peat fire, a very unsatisfactory source of illumination. Danny could make out little of her companion beyond his pale face, which looked disembodied in the darkness. Frank slowly untangled his legs and leaned forward in his chair. When he reached across to take her hand, she let him.

There was a soft scratching at the front door. Cam Liddle, having trouble with the lock, Danny thought, but when the door opened, Kerry entered, holding the credit card he'd used to finesse the latch.

"Forgot my key," he said.

CHAPTER SIXTEEN

"Give the hero and heroine plenty of alone time."
—*Camelot Guide to Romance Writing*

Danny awoke the next morning with a slight hangover and a mighty desire for rain. Not a soft rain either. A hard, driving rain. Sheets and sheets of it. Or a fog. Anything that would cancel the cruise to Ashford Castle. She struggled from bed, pulled back her window curtains, and found the sunniest of mornings. More disappointments awaited her. She'd overslept. It was too late to have a private cup of coffee and a precious hour with her journal. Too late almost for breakfast.

She showered and dressed and hurried to the breakfast room, an elegant little space with two walls of small-paned windows, one overlooking a garden and one the building's interior hallway. Inside Danny found her brother and Frank and a mild compensation for her suffering: Kerry's hangover was far worse than her own. So bad in fact—coffee only, no full Irish breakfast, no dry toast even—that Danny thought it might serve her better than any wild weather.

But no. Kerry was adamant that they keep their appointment with Donal Conneely. Mrs. Liddle alone detained them, delayed them rather, by insisting that the trio bundle up before venturing onto the water. Danny had a sweater that almost matched Frank's famous black one for bulk. She and Frank both had windbreakers, too, but Kerry had brought nothing heavier than his all-purpose blazer. When Mrs. Liddle learned that, she outfitted him with a fishing coat of stiff, waxed cloth, its pockets so big that even a bottle of poteen could disappear within one.

Conneely was bundled up as well. That is to say, the old man had added a flat woolen cap to his ensemble of the night before. They found him standing on the stone dock behind the lodge, smoking a cigarette far shorter than his very sharp nose. Danny expected him to abandon the fragment at their approach, but Conneely only removed it long enough for him to be introduced to Frank. Then he placed the cigarette stub back in his mouth, where it stayed throughout the process of boarding the boat.

A launch, Conneely had called it during his sales pitch. The vague term had suggested to Danny something long and sleek and capacious. The reality was an open metal craft little bigger than the fishing boats that lay on the shingle on either side of the dock. Its outboard was reassuringly large, but so scarred from rough treatment that little of its original paint remained. The engine's operator, an elf of a man Conneely introduced as Lal, had been handled about as gently as his machine, his damage being a smashed nose, a ragged ear, and a head almost as devoid of hair as Harty Doan's, which Lal displayed when he removed his cap to Danny. That gesture was the extent of Lal's social skills. He made no effort to help with the distribution of the human cargo, leaving it entirely to Conneely. The guide placed Danny on the narrow forward thwart, Kerry and Frank amidships, and himself astern, beside the little captain, to whom he signaled his readiness to depart by tossing the last glowing ember of his cigarette into the water.

Lal started the outboard with a single pull, and they set off at a very leisurely pace.

"We'll be crossing the lake at its widest point," Conneely said, "a trip of almost six miles."

"And as many hours," Danny heard Frank whisper. She

turned, and he smiled at her, the smile flashing in the sunlight. Kerry's face was nearly as white, and they'd yet to clear the shelter of the jetty. Once safely beyond Mrs. Liddle's authority, he'd taken off the fishing jacket, carrying it over his shoulder as jauntily as one could carry that very inflexible garment. Now he had it about him like a cape, and buttoned at the neck.

Danny zippered her own jacket as they departed the inlet and felt the full force of the wind, coming at them across the water from Cong. She heard Lal open the throttle and, sometime later, felt an answering surge from the launch. Frank had been pointing out Oughterard to Kerry. He interrupted himself to whisper to Danny, "Make that five hours."

Conneely spoke out above the engine noise and the whispering. "There are three hundred and sixty-five islands in the lough, one for each day of the year. But there are more rocks, submerged and almost submerged, than any man can count. More than Lal here can remember, though he was baptized with this very water. So keep your eyes open and sing out if you see anything jagged."

That got Frank and Danny's attention directed away from the launch and its shortcomings. Kerry had been looking outward for some time, staring at the glittering water as though he might dive in at any moment.

"Would you care for tea?" Conneely asked. Without waiting for an answer, he began rooting around in the basket beneath Frank's seat. He extracted a glass bottle, a former soda bottle, now filled with milky tea. Insulation was provided by the outer garment the bottle wore: an old striped sock. Though rustic, the system was effective. The tin cup Frank passed forward to Danny was warm to her touch.

"If you brought that bottle of yours," Conneely said to Kerry, "we can hot this up even more." The pallid younger Furey thought so little of the idea that he wouldn't nod or shake his head, wouldn't even accept a cup of unspiked tea.

Undeterred by the rebuff, Conneely shifted the topic to the lake itself. "Lough Corrib is one of the great sporting lakes of Ireland. Salmon, brown trout, and pike. Infamous pike, a gift of the monks, whose ruined abbey you saw in Cong yesterday. St. Fechin established the original monastery only a hundred years or so after Patrick's time. It was later rebuilt as an abbey by Turlough O'Connor, High King of Ireland. But I was speaking of the fish. The learned brothers introduced pike to the lake back in ancient days, and the native varieties have been fighting for space ever since. If you're ever looking for a metaphor for this poor invaded country and her troubles, you need look no further than the fishery of Lough Corrib."

The mention of invasion led him naturally to a discussion of the region's political history. It was a long discussion that featured the O'Flahertys, the clan whose ruined castles bordered the lake and dotted its islands. "You saw one such island bastion yesterday on your drive to Cong," the guide said in an aside, trying to interest Kerry in the lecture, but in vain.

The English were only just arriving on the scene as Lal steered them around one of the larger islands and Ashford Castle, a sprawling, much crenellated building, came into view. Conneely summarized the remainder of his history lesson, doing so rapid a job that he left the impression the great nineteenth century migration had been the work of Oliver Cromwell, the monster.

"And there's Ashford Castle now," Conneely calmly announced as though the place hadn't been in sight and growing for many minutes. "You *Quiet Man* devotees will recognize it as the backdrop for the movie's opening credits. The great building you see was constructed of stout. By that I meant it was built, or rather rebuilt, in the last century as the private country house of one of the Guinness heirs, Lord Ardilaun. He chose a

Gothic style, or his architect did, perhaps in homage to the original manor house that stood on the site, which dated from 1715."

There were handsome docks near the hotel for day-excursion boats from Galway, one of which was tied up now, bright green and decked like a wedding cake. Private craft, cruisers and sailboats, were also accommodated with an impressive number of slips. Lal bypassed all these facilities, steering for a humble wooden dock at the far end of the hotel's seawall. A man stood waiting for them there who, for stature, might have been Lal's brother.

That was Danny's initial impression. When they drew close enough for the novelist to toss the man their bow line, she saw that he was nothing like the boatman, being delicate in feature and genteel in dress. He was also more helpful, handing out Kerry and Danny and taking the picnic hampers Frank passed him. He did it all efficiently and quietly. Not a word spoken except when he'd been spoken to.

The last to disembark was Donal Conneely. "Have your fishing then," he said to Lal. "And the best of luck with it. But be back here at two sharp if you have to cut loose Jonah's own whale to make it."

Touching the brim of his cap, Lal backed his boat up, the outboard gurgling with the struggle. Then he was away in a puff of blue smoke.

CHAPTER SEVENTEEN

"Divide your heroine's attention between business and him."
—*Camelot Guide to Romance Writing*

Conneely introduced his new assistant as Jeffrey. "A bellhop at the Ashford Castle Hotel man and boy for fifty-two years. He was just beginning his time here when John Ford and his troupe descended on the place. Jeffrey met many celebrities in his long career, but nothing equaled that first brush with Hollywood, which he's relived over the years for countless grateful American tourists."

Jeffrey bobbed his head frequently during this abbreviation of his life, deferring to Conneely completely, though he was far better dressed—in tan slacks, salmon-colored blazer, white shirt, striped tie, and tan cap—than the tour guide and much more recently shaved. Only Jeffrey's shoes let down the side. They were running shoes older than Conneely's shirt.

As the party climbed the stairs from the seawall to a broad, manicured lawn whose centerpiece was a breeze-blown fountain, Jeffrey spoke for himself in a faint, almost querulous voice, relating the stories that had made so many tourists grateful.

"John Wayne was a big man, a big man, so he was. None of the beds in the hotel were big enough, long enough, you know, to hold him. They had to bring in a carpenter to lengthen one so the poor man could get his rest. That tickled the director, Mr. Ford, the director, as I said, so much that he put something in the movie about it, so he did."

"Right," Kerry said, all but laughing. He had been reborn the moment his foot touched dry land, casting off his borrowed coat and the greater part of his hangover, and he was at Jeffrey's elbow now, drinking in every word. "When Wayne's showing off his cottage to the Playfairs, a bed gets delivered. Wayne says it's the biggest one he could find."

" 'Is that a bed or a parade ground?' " Danny contributed. She was that pleased to see her brother so revived.

So was Conneely, who caught Danny's eye and winked.

Jeffrey's next few tidbits triggered no such associations, being about Maureen O'Hara and what a great lady she was. "The maids found Miss O'Hara's bed made every morning before they ever got to it, so they told me. And the dinner waiters, who served her of an evening, they checked her tablecloth for crumbs between courses and never found one. Victor McLaglen's cloth now, that was a state. It looked like he'd cut his meat and bread with a saw, the waiters told me. A saw for wood."

They were the memories of a bellhop, Danny reflected as her attention began to wander. She imagined Conneely introducing them to a bootblack next, who would tell them all about the half soles on Barry Fitzgerald's brogues.

"He was as bad on the set with his table manners. The poor canteen girl told me that, God rest her."

"That's enough of that," Conneely commanded. "Open the door now."

They had arrived at the entrance to the hotel. Danny noted the delicate carving of the twisted rope motif in the stone around the front door—a hundred years old and unworn—the gleaming brass nameplate, the heavy woodwork of the door itself and its frame, both varnished like church pews.

Jeffrey fell silent as they stepped inside. Indeed they all did. The lobby commanded silence and commanded it silently, with a haughty look. There was something of a church feel about the place, with its arched ceiling supported by a tracery of beams, its wood-paneled walls, confessional phone booths, and high altar of a registration desk.

From behind that busy station, a single sleek clerk was watching them suspiciously. Or so it seemed to Danny, her natural self-consciousness electrified by these posh new surroundings. She somehow transmitted the feeling to Frank, who ran a hand through his corkscrewed hair. Or perhaps that was a response to the very well-dressed hotel guests, several of whom sat reading in leather chairs that had never held a wet fisherman.

Kerry alone was unaffected by the unwelcoming chill. He hurried from one grouping of framed photographs to the next, looking for movie stars. He'd found only one relevant photo, a black and white of Victor McLaglen cradling a pint glass in his massive hand, before Conneely ushered them all outside.

"You noticed that clerk, I'm sure," Conneely said to Danny. "With your writer's sensitivity you had to. The one with the hair like a raven's wing and a heart as black, to judge by the eye he cast on us. The hotel offers its own *Quiet Man* tours, you see, and they're that jealous of freelancers like myself. I tell you this in simple frankness. If you'd prefer to take their tour, I'll understand. It's your vacation, after all. You have to make the best of it. I can wait for you on the dock."

"No way," answered Kerry, who had overheard every word. "You brought us here. We'll stick with you."

"I thank you," Conneely said, his hat over his heart.

At the guide's direction, they had left the lunch hampers at the top of the seawall. Frank volunteered himself and Danny to retrieve them now, over Kerry's token objections. Danny thought the Irishman might take her hand again, but he was only after her ear.

"You should go for that official tour," he said. "All you'll get from Conneely is blather."

"Blather," Danny said, "is exactly what my brother wants."

Returning, they found Conneely and Kerry near an elderly Volkswagen Beetle. The two were standing on opposite sides of the car, whose paint was as white as chalk and no more lustrous.

"Where's Jeffrey?" Frank asked.

"He had some business of his own to attend to," Conneely said. "But he'll be back, never fear. Until then, he's lent us this fine car so I won't be wearing you out with our roving."

Frank took the wheel again, Conneely having demurred. "When I drive, I drive, and when I talk, I talk," the guide had said. "I can't do both."

The drive was easy duty, nothing like the marathon of the previous day. They never exceeded thirty on the well-paved but narrow lanes of the estate, driving with the windows rolled down, Kerry and Danny very snug in the back. They visited the house of Red Will Danaher, Kerry pointing first to the very window in which Maureen O'Hara had cried to beat the rain, then to the little forecourt where McLaglen had given his grudging blessing to his sister's courtship, and finally to the wall over which she'd spied on Wayne. The American continued spotting things as they resumed their drive: the pasture where Wayne had ridden his black hunter, for instance, and the road down which Ward Bond, the parish priest, had made his first entrance. Conneely took no offense at being upstaged. Like Danny, he seemed to take pleasure in Kerry's pleasure.

They made one more stop before lunch, at the little stone-steepled church where Wayne had spoken his first bold words to O'Hara after mass. Conneely revealed that it was no Catholic church at all, but a Church of Ireland chapel that had once served Lord Ardilaun's household. In addition to being theologically jumbled, the place was locked, so they didn't tarry there. They were hungry, and the day was flying. Conneely directed

Danny through lefts and rights until they came to a grove of beech trees.

"It was here," the guide said, "that John Wayne caught his first glimpse of Maureen O'Hara as she was tending her sheep. She herded them right through here, up this gentle rise."

"Barefoot, the fool," Danny added for Frank's amusement.

They spread blankets they'd found in Jeffrey's trunk upon that same gentle rise. There Conneely directed the unpacking of the two baskets. One held hot foods—warm foods now and barely that—two splendid meat and potato pies and loaves of crusty bread. The other basket held the cold: bottles of Chablis, a plastic tub of salad, and a boxed layer cake.

Remembering the tea they'd been served on their voyage, Danny had been expecting rough sandwiches and rougher drink. She attempted to compliment Conneely, but the old man would have none of it.

"The thanks should go to your brother. 'Spare no expense,' he said. 'Only make it a special day.' I've seldom seen the like of his liberality. No, not even among you Yanks."

Not content with having funded the feast, Kerry provided the entertainment, telling Conneely the story of their escape from Harty Doan, reenacting as much as telling. The guide enjoyed the epic, but its heroine, Danny, did not. She moved from Kerry's neighborhood midway through the performance, relocating to the small blanket that Frank had claimed for his own.

From that moment on, Danny's enjoyment of the lunch increased appreciably. She was conscious, very conscious, of Frank's physical presence in a way she hadn't been before, not in the abbey at Cong, not even in the lounge of Liddle's the prior evening. It was more than the smell of his cologne and the tingle of his hair on her cheek as he leaned close to refill her wine glass. Her senses were heightened to an amazing degree. She could feel the warmth of him, but that was the least of it.

Without looking at him, she could sense the shape of him in the way the breeze curved itself to pass around him, could almost hear the molecules of air breaking apart on one side of him and coming back together with a million musical snaps on the other.

She almost sighed when Conneely began the packing up, getting to her feet very reluctantly to help.

"We've just time to return the car and make our rendezvous with Lal," the old man told her. "It's the shame of the ages to cut this picnic short, but the soul cannot live without sorrow. So I'm told and so I've found."

Chapter Eighteen

"In romantic suspense, forces outside the love story
must thrust it forward."
—Camelot Guide to Romance Writing

Jeffrey awaited them in the hotel parking lot. As Frank was setting the Beetle's hand brake, Conneely addressed them sidemouthed: "I've settled up with Jeffrey for the car and his time, of course. But you might want to throw in something for his stories. A tip, as it were."

He then vacated his seat very quickly for a man his age. Jeffrey was about to dispose of a cigarette he'd only recently lit. Conneely relieved him of it and set off toward the lake and the waiting Lal in his usual rolling stride. Frank left the Fureys as well, after asking Jeffrey where a bathroom might be found and receiving in reply a vague gesture in the direction of the ornate hotel.

Danny busied herself with the unloading of the Volkswagen's peculiar trunk. The job of tipping its owner she left to the still-euphoric Kerry, with the expectation that it would be done, or overdone, quickly. Jeffrey, it seemed, was expecting the same dispatch. Only Kerry, leaning comfortably against a chalky fender, was in no apparent hurry.

"So, Jeff," he said. "Thought of any more stories?"

Jeffrey began to mumble something about McLaglen's openhandedness, perhaps intending it to be instructive as well as entertaining. Kerry cut him short. "We've had enough of the standard-issue tourist stuff. The thing is, we're researching a book. We need something juicier."

"Juicier?" Jeffrey repeated, conveying the term's foreignness to him by mimicking Kerry's New Jersey pronunciation.

"You know, racier. These people were Hollywood stars after all, a pretty racy bunch. What was going on after hours at the hotel? Who was sleeping with whom? Are you sure Maureen O'Hara was making her own bed ever morning or just not unmaking it at night?"

"Miss O'Hara was a married woman," said the bellhop, scandalized.

Kerry backed away from that icon carefully. "Of course she was. But what about the others? What were they up to when no one was looking?"

Jeffrey somehow lit a cigarette while continually shaking his head. "I was just a lad then, so I was. I never worked at night. And the staff, the staff would never repeat things in front of us youngers. Not things like that. Never."

Kerry asked, "What about that poor canteen girl? Donal cut you off when you mentioned her. What was her name and what's her story?"

Danny had forgotten that tidbit and Conneely's reaction to it. She stopped what she'd been doing—repacking one of the hampers—and gave the conversation her full attention.

Jeffery drew deeply at his cigarette, and his next words came out with the smoke. "They wouldn't talk about the death of that girl in front of me. That especially, not even with me asking about it every day."

"Death?" Kerry repeated. A practiced interviewer, he was able to dampen down his interest.

But however flat its tone, Kerry's question put Jeffrey on his guard. "T'was nothing," he said. "An accident."

Danny rejoined them. "What kind of accident?"

"You'll miss your boat if you don't hurry along. Mr. Conneely will be coming back after you, so he will."

Kerry took his wallet from the breast pocket of his blazer and from it extracted two banknotes of unequal size, a humble five euro note and a larger ten. The five he handed to Jeffrey. The tenner he held in his hand.

"Thanks for your time," he said. "And for the stories. They were great. I can't wait to watch the movie again, now that I've seen this place."

"You're welcome I'm sure," the bellhop replied. He was studying his cigarette. Pretending to study it, Danny thought, but actually watching the bill move languidly in Kerry's hand. "If there's anything else I can do for you. . . ."

"Nothing else," Kerry said. "Unless it's that story about the accident. You say the girl had some connection to *The Quiet Man?*"

Jeffrey turned sharply about to face the hotel as though his name had been shouted by the pile of stone itself. He slowly turned back to the Fureys and tipped his cap.

"I'll just be off then." He opened the door of his car, shooing Kerry from its fender with the motion. "Thank you for your kind attention."

They watched him drive away, Danny saying, "Amazing, your powers of persuasion."

Kerry was tucking the banknote into his shirt pocket as though it were a tissue. "Welcome to the real world, Sis. You can put dialogue into your characters' mouths. I have to wheedle."

Frank returned then, and he and Danny carried their lightened loads down the seawall stairs to the humble wooden dock, where Conneely and his launch awaited them. Danny expected Kerry to accost the guide regarding the story that Jeffrey had withheld, but once inside the boat—covered once more by his borrowed sea jacket—Kerry lapsed into silence.

The return voyage should have been shorter—the wind was now behind them—or at least it should have seemed shorter, in the manner of return trips everywhere, but to Danny, it was endless. The following wind blew exhaust fumes the full length of the boat, and the motion of the vessel was equally unpleasant. What had been an invigorating bounce on the outbound leg was now a slow rollercoaster ride, the morning's crisp little waves having given way to a miniature oily swell. Danny found herself thinking involuntarily of meat pie, Chablis, and layer cake, and even tasting them. She looked to Conneely for some diversion, but the old man was staring very fixedly at the horizon, as were Kerry and Frank. Only Lal seemed unaffected, luckily, or they might have wandered among the little islands forever.

In recognition of this fidelity, Kerry tipped Lal mightily when they were standing safe and dry on Liddle's stony shore. The boatman accepted their thanks in his phlegmatic way, saluted Conneely, and sailed off.

"Are you up for White o' Morn tomorrow?" the guide asked, still waving. "Or do you need a day of rest?"

"Tomorrow's a long way off," Kerry said. "I'm thinking about dinner."

"Please," his sister said. "I've just this moment stopped thinking about lunch."

"Can you recommend a good restaurant in Galway, Donal?"

"Certainly I can. The Eyre House is always reliable. Or Hooker Jimmy's if you like seafood."

"No fish," Frank said emphatically.

"If you'd like some music with your comestibles, traditional Irish music that is, I'd suggest the Abbey on Flood Street. Not fancy at all, but good."

"You like the place yourself?" Kerry asked.

"I do."

"Then join us. We can talk about tomorrow over dessert."

Danny, who had absented herself from the conversation, attempted to intrude now, all too late, Conneely's "I'd be delighted" trumping her soundly. The guide turned down Kerry's further offer of a ride into the city, proposed a meeting time of seven, and ushered them to the lodge path.

Once inside the building itself, Danny opened her mouth to speak again, only to have her line trodden upon by Frank. "Are you that fond of the man that you have to have all your meals with him?"

"Explain it to him, Danny," Kerry said.

"Me?"

"Sorry. I thought you were up with me for once. It's all about an accident story Jeffrey mentioned but wouldn't tell. A fatality connected with the movie company. I want to ask Conneely about it in a setting where he can't tip his hat and dematerialize."

Frank asked, "What makes you think Conneely knows anything about it?"

"He stopped Jeffrey from telling us. And he promised us stories about the movie known only to God. Maybe this is one he's been saving. Maybe that's why Jeffrey wouldn't elaborate."

"He wouldn't elaborate," Danny returned, "because the story involves the rock and anchor of his life, the hotel. You saw the way he looked at the place when you were egging him on. God help him if he ever had to choose between Ashford Castle and Maureen O'Hara."

"God help any man in that dilemma," her brother replied.

CHAPTER NINETEEN

"The best conflicts grow more conflicted over time."
— *Camelot Guide to Romance Writing*

The music provided by the Abbey Restaurant was traditional, but the interior decoration was not. Danny's view included a very abstract painting, a war of blues and reds in which the only discernible object was a claw, or something very like a claw, in the painting's upper third. It seemed poised to strike down at the white head of Donal Conneely, who sat opposite Danny and therefore was the novelist's proper study. But Danny found the old man's keen gray eyes more disturbing than the jumbled painting and avoided them.

Conneely had been telling the table of the year or so he'd spent in Philadelphia, Pennsylvania. Now he'd arrived at the point of his tale, his reason for returning to Ireland.

"It was the openness of the place. The terrible openness, as I came to think of it."

"Of Philadelphia?" Max asked, for he had deigned to join them for dinner. "Are you sure you weren't in Montana?"

In a trout stream? Danny asked without moving her lips. Max had gone on and on about those on the drive to the city, belaboring the superiority of the Montana streams to the Connemara ones. From that—and from the fact that he and Cam Liddle were planning a return to the lough for the following day—Danny had concluded that Max's latest outing had not been a triumph.

"I'm not talking about physical space, Mr. Alnutt," Conneely protested. "I'm discussing psychic space, if anything. The blank slate quality of the country and the people who lived there. It's the very reason poor souls have always flocked to America, I know, the chance to start afresh in a place with no history to speak of. But I missed the jumble of Ireland's history, the crushing weight of it, some might say. I felt like a creature of the ocean depths suddenly brought up to the airy surface. I had the bends, the spiritual bends, if you follow me. It was the difference between living in a land where anything might happen and one in which everything has happened.

"But it was more than that. I was afraid I was losing my personal history, that my past was in danger of untangling itself, of becoming a straight simple line that led directly to this new beginning. I didn't want to give up my past. Didn't want it demoted to preamble. So I came back."

The explanation puzzled Danny but it seemed to please Frank, reminding him of his own experience of meeting with too many straight answers in Boston, which he now recounted for Conneely. Soon the two of them were chatting away like old friends, Kerry and Max joining in when possible and Danny sinking back into her accustomed role of odd woman out.

She was tired as well. While Frank and Kerry had spent the last of the afternoon napping, she had walked the lakeshore, thinking over their day. As a result, she was now so fatigued that she barely tasted the Abbey's specialty, leg of lamb in gooseberry sauce, the slices served upright like runic stones, supported by a mound of garlic mashed potatoes.

When the dinner plates had been cleared away, Kerry very casually said, "Your friend Jeffrey mentioned something in passing today. A death connected with *The Quiet Man* production."

Conneely shook his head. "The old dark rumors," he said.

"There are few left who remember them. Jeffrey would be one, of course. But I doubt he knows much of the story, as he was just a boy then, with never a crack in his heart."

They ordered coffee from a waitress who breezed by, all but Max, who ordered a brandy. Conneely licked his lips at that, so Kerry promptly ordered a second for him. On the other side of the large room, the musicians were playing a reel. Yet another reel to Danny, on whom all reels were wasted. The tour guide bobbed his head in time with the happy music until Kerry nudged him verbally.

"About this story."

"A sad, sordid thing," Conneely said, waving a hand dismissively. "It reflects no credit on this land, nor on the movie you love so much. For the sake of that love, you should put the rumors out of your mind."

The waitress reappeared, and the old man took his snifter gratefully, toasting his hosts with it before drinking.

"Of course," he said after carefully wiping his lips with his hand, "as a selling point for your *Quiet Man* book, this true story would serve much better than a simple rehashing of a movie, however famous."

This last was delivered to Danny together with an accusing look. Danny passed the look in turn to Kerry, who said, "I may have mentioned our book idea in the pub last night. To explain our interest."

"It's interesting a publisher that's your real challenge," Conneely opined. "A sordid tale is always good for that."

"Good in general," Max said.

He was swirling his brandy with a will. Conneely eschewed this affectation, warming his glass instead between his wrinkled hands. Danny wondered how much warmth was left in them.

Aloud, she said, "Let's have the details."

Conneely, who had put his glass down to applaud the musicians, replied, "The details, is it? Why, the details are unknown. That's what gives the story what interest it has. It's only in your very minor stories that everything is worked out. Your high art, like your real life, is all questions.

"You might answer a few of them in this case—one might answer them—but it would mean solving a genuine mystery. And that in turn may mean braving a wee bit of danger."

"Danger?" Kerry asked.

"Of course. There's danger behind every unopened door, and there are unopened doors aplenty in the sad tale of Bridey Finnerman."

Conneely sat staring into what remained of his brandy for a time. At length, he said, "As best I can recall, it happened like this. When they were making *The Quiet Man,* they moved all over the Connemara Peninsula, getting as far out as Clifden, on the very tip, and up into Mayo as well. To feed the actors and the technicians, they set up a mobile commissary, a kitchen on wheels. In a trailer, it was, pulled by a truck. They hired local women to fix the food and serve it, and one of these was Bridey Finnerman.

"She was a young girl, right out of school, and movie-struck, as schoolgirls often are. She traveled many miles by bus each day just to be near the people from Hollywood and serve them their tea.

"That much is common knowledge. That and a bit more. Just before the filming ended, Bridey was struck and killed late one night on the road between Cong and Ashford Castle, many miles from her home village."

Conneely paused then to refresh himself and to look each of his listeners in the eye in turn. Satisfied, he continued. "The car that killed the girl was never identified, an amazing thing, when you stop to think of it. There were few cars in the west of Ireland in the fifties and fewer places to have a damaged one repaired.

But the police never found the juggernaut, nor did they ever explain the girl's presence on the road that night. Her death was ruled an accident after an investigation many of the locals considered perfunctory at best.

"There the facts end and the speculation begins. And of all the cottage industries in this land of cottage industries, speculating is the most widespread."

He lifted his snifter to his lips again, but it was empty. Kerry signaled for another, and Conneely, accepting this sign of good faith, struck on.

"Most of the speculation has involved Bridey's brother Seamus. He was a ne'er-do-well farmer back in 1951. But within a year of his sister's death, Finnerman sold his rocky little holding and bought a fine house. A squire's house. The source of his sudden wealth was another mystery. It wasn't his sister's insurance, as she'd had none. But there was talk of monthly letters from America."

Kerry had been sitting on his tongue, so to speak, but he could do it no longer. "Finnerman was blackmailing somebody. Some American. He knew who had killed his sister."

"You're leaping the brook," Conneely said, "when there are stones you might walk across. Listen now. There was talk of a diary kept by Bridey in which she described her time in the limelight. I happen to know the source of this piece of the tale, and I'm fairly confident of it. So confident that I'm tempted to move it from the speculation column altogether. This diary may be the source of Seamus Finnerman's secret power. In it, the girl may have described something that befell her or something she witnessed or overheard. The diary might even confirm the rumor, the very sad rumor, that she was with child at the time of her death."

He drank from his newly arrived snifter then. Drank so deeply that Danny knew the storytelling was almost over.

"The letters from America were said to have stopped in the early seventies. Since then Finnerman has become a miser and a recluse and all he built up has gone to rack and to ruin. So far as I know, he still lives in that crumbling house of his, out west beyond the lake we crossed today.

"He certainly fits the title of your favorite movie, you Fureys. *The Quiet Man.* Whether he's had his dead sister for company all these years and whether she's been a comfort to him or a scourge, no one can say."

Conneely was staring at the table, his brows casting wild shadows over his eyes. "Few men have been given more time to repent their sins," he said. "God grant he's used every minute."

CHAPTER TWENTY

"Give your heroine interests beyond romance."
—Camelot Guide to Romance Writing

The Americans and Frank sat in silence for a long while after Conneely had finished his tale, out of respect for the telling certainly but also in response to Conneely's own emotional reaction. It appeared to Danny to be one of extreme regret. Without lifting his eyes from the tabletop, the old man shook his white head, moved his lips wordlessly, and shook his head again. He seemed sincerely sorry that he'd given up his story. But why?

Conneely didn't stay long enough to explain. He barely stayed through his own good-bye, rising during the course of it and stepping behind Kerry's chair on his way to the door.

Kerry twisted in his seat to address him. "What about tomorrow? You're going to meet us, right?"

"Sure, sure," Conneely said, blurring the soft words together. "Look for me in Oughterard proper about nine." He then hurried out, his normal strut reduced to a shamble.

To Danny's relief, Kerry immediately announced that he was also ready to go. Her brother was pleased with himself, she could tell, and pleased with how his dinner party had come off. But he saved all his chortling for the privacy of the Ford. Max had grabbed the front passenger seat for himself and promptly fallen asleep, and the ensuing conversation was whispered to the accompaniment of his snoring.

"It's perfect," Kerry said when they were safely on the Oughterard road. "This story. It's better than I hoped. It's exactly what we need for our book."

Danny said nothing. Her window rolled down and her head half out in the slipstream, she was breathing in air that was like a cure after the smoke and heat of the restaurant.

Frank took her place in the conversation and her role: the voice of reason. "What story? As Conneely admitted himself, it's a fishnet of a story. Mostly holes."

"If it's a fishnet," Kerry said dreamily, "we'll just have to catch something in it." He began humming a song from their dinner concert, using Max's snores as his base line. He must have been thinking away as he hummed, however, for when the musical interlude ended, he said, "Let's recap what we know. A beautiful young girl gets a job with the movie company."

"You've already exceeded what you know," Frank interrupted. "Conneely never once mentioned her looks."

"For the purposes of this summation," Kerry replied, "she's beautiful. Beautiful but naive."

Danny pulled her head in from the slipstream long enough to ask, "Who's the romance writer now?"

Frank, seated in front of her, half turned to say, "Roll up your window. You'll give your brother pneumonia. And help me watch the road. Sometimes the cows get out at night. You'll not see a black one till its hamburger on the windscreen."

"Beautiful *and* naive," Kerry said again to reorient them. "Her name is Bridey Finnerman. She's dreamt of the movies all her life and now she's landed in one. Or next to one. At a critical moment for her psychologically. The first blush of womanhood, you might say."

"*You* might say," Danny rejoined.

"Bridey falls in love with some man from the movie company.

117

Maybe an actor she's read about in her movie magazines. Or maybe he's one of the crew, someone who promises to make her a star. Bridey believes the guy when he says he'll take her away to sunny California. She becomes the mistress of this Mr. X. They slip away during lulls in the shooting. Maybe even spend a weekend somewhere cozy. Everything's idyllic until Bridey discovers she's pregnant. She demands a wedding and pretty damn quick.

"Mr. X puts her off, maybe even tries to talk her into slipping over to the continent for an abortion. She won't hear of it. Their scenes become more and more combative, more and more indiscreet. Mr. X knows he may be only one outburst away from a terrible scandal.

"One night Bridey makes the mistake of coming to Ashford Castle for a final showdown with Mr. X. She's desperate. She wants an answer. Unbeknownst to her, Mr. X has learned of her plan. He lies in wait for her with a car and runs her down. The poor kid."

Kerry stopped there, though whether he was affected by his own fairy tale or by the thought that it might not be a fairy tale Danny couldn't say. The moment was ripe, psychologically ripe, for her rebuttal, but she lapsed once more into silence. The cudgels were again taken up by Frank.

"How long were these movie people in Ireland, anyway? Eh?" This last prompt was to Danny, Kerry having shrugged into the rearview mirror.

"I don't know," she said cautiously. "I haven't done the research. It must have been a span of weeks."

"It would have to have been a span of months," Frank said, "for the girl to have realized she was pregnant."

Kerry said, "So she only suspects."

"Why didn't the doctor who performed Bridey's postmortem discover it? Donal said the police could never say why she was on that road. If they'd known she was pregnant, they would have had a fair idea. And why kill the girl in the first place? Why not just marry her and dump her six months later in the accepted Hollywood fashion?"

"That's an easy one," Kerry said. "Mr. X was already married. No way out there."

"All right, what about this mystery car? Why was it never found?"

Kerry was answering before Frank had finished asking. "The murderer hid it in a truck the film company was using to haul their equipment around. He could have slipped it right out of the country that way."

"With none of the other movie people noticing?" Frank asked. "Or are you proposing a massive conspiracy? Maybe Bridey was sleeping with every man in the cast."

"That would be better," Danny said. "For the plot of a story, I mean. More suspects."

Her brother said, "This isn't a story. Maybe the murderer pushed the car into the lough. It's down there to this day, snagging fishing lines."

"Then why did no one notice the car was missing? If there weren't many cars around back then, it would have been no great job for the police to account for them all."

"Help me out here, Sis. This guy's logic is relentless. Give me the professional treatment on this automobile problem."

"I'm a romance writer, not a crime writer," Danny said. "Besides, I'm on the lookout for black cows." They were well away from the city now, and the road was darker than any she'd driven in New Jersey.

"I'm on the cow watch," Frank said. "Go ahead. If you were writing this, how would you handle the car?"

"I don't know," she said, but the words were transformed by her tone into "let me see."

"The murder car would have to have belonged to the murderer or at least to the production company. A stolen car would have been reported. The movie people probably rented a number of cars for ferrying the actors around and odd jobs. If I were writing it, I'd make them all the same car, the same make, model, and year. The same color, too. That would have been natural enough, especially if cars were so rare in the west of Ireland in 1951 that they had to be hired in Dublin or shipped over from England with the rest of the movie equipment.

"I'd have the police check the production company's cars, but I'd have it done by some country constable who was in awe of the Hollywood types, deferential even. It would be easy to fool someone like that. You could show him an undamaged car, have him check it off his list, then show him the same car later after you'd switched its license plate with the one from the murder car. He'd report he'd seen two cars, both undamaged."

"You're back to a conspiracy involving the whole movie company," Frank objected.

"Only the murderer and the guy responsible for maintaining the cars," Danny said. "If the car guy is the murderer, you're only talking about one man."

"There'd have been drivers, too," Frank said. "They wouldn't have had Wayne and O'Hara driving themselves around Connemara."

"He's right," Kerry said. "There's this whole black cow issue."

"So one of the drivers is fired by the car guy for some trumped-up reason. Or sent on a fool's errand by train."

"Why would this car guy—"

"Call him Mr. Y," Kerry suggested.

"—help the murderer in the first place?"

"I'll handle that one," Kerry said, waving his hand in the air like a schoolboy. "Mr. Y doesn't know Mr. X is a murderer. No one's talking murder. The police are investigating a hit-and-run. Mr. X tells Mr. Y that it was all an accident. He doesn't want to land in an Irish jail over an accident."

"Well done," Frank conceded. "That would explain why the car wasn't identified right away. But why was it never found?"

"We don't know enough yet to say," Danny said.

Frank liked her "yet" not at all. "Don't tell me you're getting interested in this legend."

He was signaling for their last turn, though there was no other car within miles or cow either.

Danny waited until they were safely in the lodge lane before replying. "It has its points of interest."

"Name one."

"Those letters from America. The ones Bridey's brother got every month. When did Conneely say they stopped coming?"

"The early seventies," Kerry said.

They were pulling into Liddle's gravel lot by then. Danny considered the timing perfect. "I happen to know that John Ford died in 1973."

CHAPTER TWENTY-ONE

"Sexual tension is the smoldering fuse
of the romantic bombshell."
—*Camelot Guide to Romance Writing*

"In Oughterard." Danny looked at the two words for a moment before adding a third and a fourth: "Perhaps forever."

She was seated in the lounge at Liddle's, journal on her lap, a plastic pot of coffee at her elbow, Kelsey, the senior Labrador, curled at her feet. The first turf blocks of the day were burning in the fireplace, courtesy of Cam Liddle, who had stoked the perpetual fire on his way to join Max on the dock. Danny had been in Ireland so long now that she didn't automatically think of the burning leaves of childhood autumns when she smelled the peat smoke. Her mind thus freed of the distant past fell into a reverie on the very recent past: their arrival home from the Abbey the night before.

They'd entered the lodge still talking of their dinner, Kerry still firing forth ideas, though visibly tired. A sleepwalking Max had passed the lounge without a pause and Frank had firmly vetoed any detour there by the Fureys. They'd parted in the hallway that divided the lake view rooms from the garden view. There Kerry had banged Danny's arm in parting and Frank had looked back at the novelist over his shoulder.

Danny thought of that look now, trying to parse it, hopelessly. It had been a look of infinite meanings and no meaning, the merest eye contact only. As she bent forward slightly to scratch Kelsey's proffered ear, Danny could only conclude that there'd been a message there, a clue, as there'd been a message in Conneely's parting regret.

Messages in Gaelic, she told herself.

With an effort, Danny pulled her gaze from the fire. She turned to the previous entry in the journal in search of some bit of work she could take up again. She had to get something done, she told herself, while this peaceful moment lasted. But Kelsey was requesting further scratching. At least that was how Danny interpreted the presence of the retriever's broad black head on her knee. She provided the service, her eyes scanning the pages of carefully written notes she'd compiled for her next book, *Beyond Tomorrow.*

She could almost hear Conneely dismissing it as "a very minor story," with all its questions neatly answered. In a silent rebuttal, Danny compared her outline to a drystone wall, the stones fitted tightly in their spaces, however ragged their exposed edges.

Tightly stacked it may have been, but *Beyond Tomorrow* couldn't hold her interest. Again and again she was drawn instead to Kerry's trial solution for the mystery of Bridey Finnerman. Before she'd even undressed for bed the night before, Danny had dismissed her brother's plot as no more than a possible red herring, something a mystery writer might use to fool a reader. A young girl run down by the lover she was coming to confront? It was the first explanation most people would think of. Therefore Danny the storyteller mistrusted it. She'd fallen asleep thinking of alternatives. And considering the rumors of the dead girl's diary. Conneely had said the diary might contain the record of something the girl had seen or overheard, and it was this hydra-headed possibility that had intrigued Danny, though not enough to keep her awake.

It intrigued her still, this diary. She was musing on it anew when Frank stepped down into the lounge.

She was aware of him immediately, although he moved almost silently on stocking feet. In truth, Danny had been expecting him, having noted that he was by habit an earlier riser, a far earlier riser, than her brother. She even expected what he did next, which was to take her nearly empty coffee cup, refill it from her pot, and sit down on her sofa. But that was as far as expecting could prepare her.

"How did you sleep?" he asked.

"Fine. And you?" This for form's sake, for she could see that he'd slept badly or, at the very least, insufficiently. His red hair was nearly as wild as Kerry's, his eyes half-opened. His left cheek, still unshaved, bore across it like a diagonal scar the mark of a pillow's seam.

"His nibs kept me up for hours last night after you'd turned in, hatching new ideas about Bridey Finnerman. He's making up for lost time now. I doubt we'll be keeping our nine o'clock appointment. I hope we don't."

"You do?" Danny asked. "Why?"

"Premonition. We have a lot of them over here. In this damp climate, you get very conversant with your bones. I've a feeling in mine right now. It's telling me to pack you three into the car and set off for this Letterfenny apparition. As hazy as that place sounds, it has to be more solid than any of this movie nonsense."

Danny waited for him to list his criticisms in detail, but he was suddenly busy with Kelsey, who had deserted her for the newcomer as soon as she decently could, and was having her ears ruffled aggressively.

"What about the book?" Danny asked. She reclaimed her cup, refilled it, and tried to hand it back.

"Your turn," he said in declining it. "No offense, but no one will miss that book, not even your brother, for all his talk about immortality. I reminded him that he has years yet to worry about that. And in any case, he's already achieved the only immortality any of us gets, the chance to live on in a heart or two.

"No more do you need a movie book for your career, as he seems to think. You're better off writing about your marriage."

"My marriage? I write romance novels. There wasn't much romance in my marriage."

"I know."

"How do you know?" She raised a mental pen, ready to record another black mark against her brother's discretion.

"From your novel, *Beyond Forever*. It's a picture of your marriage. Or I should say, a photographic negative of it. Everything reversed: blacks white, voids full to overflowing. Passion where there wasn't even love, grand gestures where there weren't little attentions."

Danny was sticking to her first guess. "What did Kerry tell you?"

It was the first time in the conversation that either of them had spoken Kerry's name. Now it worked as an invocation. An evil invocation, as far as their quiet moment was concerned. For the man himself walked in on the heels of it.

"Morning, guys. Morning, dog. The shower felt good. You two had breakfast yet? Let's get going. We've got a big day ahead of us. I feel it in my bones."

"That's the damp," Danny said.

They'd set a time for meeting Donal Conneely but not a specific place, an omission Frank mentioned more than once during their hasty breakfast. Neither Furey was worried, Kerry because of his confidence regarding the day's success and Danny because she'd come to think of Conneely as the type of penny that would always turn up.

He hadn't turned up by nine, so they drove into town, slowly, through a mist as thick as a fog. They found Conneely standing in front of the Oughterard Hotel, smoking one of his truncated cigarettes, oblivious to the weather. Danny made room for him by joining Kerry in the backseat, and the old man climbed in beside Frank, smelling of witch hazel and very wet wool.

"Good morning to you all," he said, beaming about him. "What a splendid car. Large and wonderfully appointed. So, where shall it take us? Will we defy the elements and visit White o' Morn? The gloom may add to the emotional resonance of the place, that shell of its former glory."

Though the Fureys hadn't conferred at breakfast regarding a change of plans, having been outnumbered by Frank and his warning bones, they spoke out now from one mind.

"About last night," Kerry said.

"That story you told us," Danny said on top of him, jumbling their words together.

"What's this now?" Conneely asked. "You're not mad at me for walking out on you surely. You'd never be upset over that trifling lapse of manners. I'd had too much brandy is all. I needed some air."

"We're not mad," Danny hastened to assure him. "We're just curious. Last night you mentioned Bridey Finnerman's diary. You said you were confident it existed. Did you mean the story came from someone you trust?"

"Someone I know, say. So many of these old stories go about with no name attached to them that just to know the source for once, to be able to tie the thing to a flesh and blood human being, is a comfort. Though I suppose you could say that I trust May O'Shaughnessy. Trust her word. But I wouldn't leave her alone with a bottle I hoped to see again. Not May."

"Who is this May?" Frank asked.

"No one important ever. A housewife, most of her life. A housemaid, once. Housemaid to Squireen Finnerman, Seamus

Finnerman, the dead girl's brother. How May came to hear of the diary, I couldn't tell you, because I've never been told myself. But she was in a position to have heard of it."

"And she's still alive?" Kerry asked. He was all but in the front seat himself, his head squeezed in between the headrests, his sister mashed into a distant corner.

"Certainly she is. That is, I think she is. I've heard no contrary reports. And I would have, recluse though she be. My contacts in this part of the country are still reliable."

"Then she lives in this area," Danny said.

"South of here and a little west. Near Screeb. Children raised and gone and her husband dead. He was a character. I could tell you a story or two about Bernie O'Shaughnessy. But I observe that we've already steamed up your windows horribly. So maybe it would be better if you told me what this quiz program is all about."

"Would she talk to us?" Danny asked. "May O'Shaughnessy?"

"Is that it? You're after the old mystery? Listen, lass, if this is because of anything I said last night, any passing remark about solving a real mystery, you should put it from your mind. I was joking with you, not tempting you. Mr. O'Shea, tell these long straight faces that I meant nothing by it."

"I have already," Frank answered. He'd done his bit for the foggy windows by rolling his down to the stop, and his words were all but lost in the sound of a tanker truck swooshing by on the wet pavement.

"I'm not saying we can solve the mystery," Danny said. "But it wouldn't hurt to hear more about it."

"But what of the cottage?" Conneely asked. "What of White o' Morn? It's in the other direction entirely. And this may decide the question for you: We won't have time to go to both places, Screeb and Maam. I've an appointment this afternoon I cannot fail to keep. Not for love nor money."

127

"We can go to Maam anytime," Kerry said. "It's no day to be touring a ruin. What do you say?"

Conneely scratched at his chin with a row of gnarled knuckles, the rasping audible above the traffic noise. "I say, I wish you'd hatched this plot last night. I could have scouted ahead a little. Suppose we drive all the way down there and she won't see us? Then what will you think of me? We should take her a little bottle of something to improve our chances. A goodwill offering. Have you that poteen of yours, young Kerry?"

"I have," he replied. "And I'm keeping it; it's my last bottle."

"Then I don't blame you a bit. Hmmm. It's early to be buying something, but give me a tenner and I'll see what I can do. You three see if you can get these windows clear."

"We're off," Kerry said when the old man had hurried away. "What do you think of that, Frank?"

"You took the words out of my mouth."

Chapter Twenty-Two

"Stretch your readers' credulity
on the rack of your imagination."
—*Camelot Guide to Romance Writing*

The O'Shaughnessy farm was some little way outside of Screeb, which, given the neglected state of the homestead, was a blessing for the village. The main house, a modest rectangle built of concrete blocks once painted white, was set close to the road and approached by a short grassy drive. Grass grew in abundance everywhere, its only competition rhododendron bushes, as tall as the Ford and crowded close around the block walls of the house, hiding their windows.

Danny parked in a little graveled space between the house and the barn, whose blocks had never been painted and were water soaked and crumbling. Though all four climbed out into the misty day, Conneely begged his clients to remain with the car. He approached the house, bottle at the ready, knocked, opened the door, and disappeared within.

"Never to be seen again," Frank said.

Staying with that ominous theme, Kerry, who was standing nearest the open door of the barn, remarked, "There's a skeleton in here."

"Any number, I should think," Danny said.

"A real one, Sis."

Danny and Frank joined him. The interior of the structure

was well lit, the roof having fallen in sometime in the recent past. Its remains, bits of rotten wood and slate, lay scattered on the dirt floor. In amongst the wreckage was the anatomical specimen to which Kerry had referred: a curving spinal column and a flat triangular skull, picked clean.

"Dog?" Kerry asked.

"Sheep," Frank said. "The silly thing must have wandered in here and caught its leg in something."

"Maybe it was in here when the roof fell," Kerry suggested.

"Maybe it was on the roof when it fell," Danny said.

The others looked at her. Danny could see that they were trying to decide if she was making a joke. She was curious on the point herself. She was feeling very much as if she'd stepped through that looking glass she'd earlier mentioned to Frank. A sheep on a rooftop seemed no more unlikely to her than a Danny Furey in a weedy Screeb barnyard, on the trail of some dead crime with a brother she barely spoke to and a man she barely knew.

Conneely was calling to them from the farmhouse doorway. "Come in. Come in, young people. She'll see you."

They entered a room whose thick atmosphere was a blend of mustiness and peat smoke. And dust. The few spare pieces of furniture showed signs of a recent wiping, and Danny wondered if Conneely had done it as part of his negotiations. The guide had left the doorway for the hearth and was attempting to persuade some of the choking haze to exit through the flue. The job of introducing the trio therefore devolved on Kerry, who had been the first across the threshold. He presented himself to the lady of the house, a figure seated by the fire, glass in hand.

May O'Shaughnessy was a large woman of sixty or more, blotched and bloated of face and red of eye, as any occupant of that smoky room must inevitably have been. Her grizzled hair was as curly as the mist had made Kerry's and showed no mark of comb or brush. Her attire, what they could see of it, consisted of an old tan raincoat, stained brown at the cuffs and hem, and calf-high rubber boots.

"Sit down," the woman said after she'd repeated each of their names a time or two.

Only one chair looked habitable, a one-armed Windsor, and Danny took it, settling herself lightly on its edge.

"Can I offer you some tea?"

Danny looked in vain for pot or cup while Frank declined on their behalf. "We've only just breakfasted, thank you."

"Just breakfasted?" May asked him. "And it ten o'clock and more. You were none of you raised on a farm."

"They're on holiday, May," Conneely said. He was rattling a chain that ran up into the chimney and might or might not have been connected to a damper. "Sweet Jesus! I think you've a dead bird up there."

Kerry added, seemingly against his will, "And there's a dead sheep in the barn."

"Gertie," May told him. "A family pet. I haven't the heart to bury her."

Conneely, eyeing Kerry reproachfully, forsook the fireplace and resumed control of the interview. "As I said, they've come to ask you about Seamus Finnerman."

May spat toward the fire. "There's for him, the miser. The less said of him, the better. I've been waiting forty years to hear he's died, and he's disappointed me every day of it."

Danny leaned even more forward. "We'd like to hear about his sister's diary."

"There's an American for you," May said to Frank. "No 'Good morning and how are your old bones, May? How are those children of yours?' Just business, first and last."

She lifted her rheumy gaze to Danny's clear one. "I know what you're here for. Didn't Mr. Conneely himself tell me?

Twenty euros. There's business for you. Twenty euros for the story."

Danny was prepared to haggle, but Kerry already had his bottomless wallet in hand.

"Don't worry," the woman told them as she stuffed the note unfolded into her pocket. "You'll get full value for your money."

The bottle of whiskey Conneely had carried in with him was nowhere in sight. May produced it now, pulling it from her left rubber boot. She refilled her glass and slipped the bottle away again.

"I worked for Seamus Finnerman back in the sixties. The early sixties. I remember I was still with him when your young president, the one they shot, came to Ireland.

"I cleaned and dusted that whole great house of his. Just me myself. It would have been too big a job for one except that no one lived there but Finnerman. The other servants, a cook and a gardener, were day workers like myself. Only Finnerman slept there, and he barely did. Barely wrinkled the covers of his bed, being too sly and secret to ever forget himself and toss them about. Too careful. Careful and quiet. Many's the time he'd come into a room where I was dusting and I'd not notice him for minutes and minutes. Then I'd catch sight of him watching me and jump."

"About the diary," Kerry said.

"I'm setting the scene for its entrance, man. Dressing the stage. You Americans. You want the body on the first page, I suppose, and the devil take the atmosphere."

"Never mind that, May," Conneely said. "Go on."

"As I was saying, it was me and a cook and a man to do the gardening. I had full charge of the house and the run of it. I could enter any room I pleased save one. A room on the first floor—you Yanks call it the second floor—at the head of the stairs. That room alone was locked and always locked.

"Naturally that locked door drew me like a moth to the electric. Hadn't I run to the cinema to see those gothic thrillers as a girl? The ones with Margaret Lockwood or—what was her name?—Patricia Roc. They always had a locked room in them and every one held some horror, like the mad wife chained up in *Jane Eyre* that Joan Fontaine found."

Another crazy movie fan, Danny thought. She guessed that Frank was thinking the same thing by the way he shuffled his feet behind her chair.

"I listened for the rattle of chains at that door often, but never heard a thing. I even asked the squire about it, whether he didn't want me to straighten up in there. He told me it was a box room and never used. But late one night, when I was hurrying home from a party, I chanced to pass the house. The two little windows over the front door, windows I knew belonged to that locked room, were glowing like owl's eyes in the night."

She paused to drink. They watched her without speaking or even moving, except for Conneely, who licked his lips.

"I was determined from that night on to get into the secret room. I tried every key I came across, but none of them fit. Then one day I chanced to be dusting the squire's desk and I chanced to look into a drawer that was slightly ajar. In it was a key I'd never seen before, an old-fashioned iron thing with a bit of ribbon tied to it.

"It happened that the master was gone to town for the post that morning, so I slipped the key from the desk and hurried myself up the stairs to the locked room, starting at every creaking tread. I put the key into the lock, and it turned almost by itself.

"I was inside the room just as easily. I found no one chained to the wall, but no box room either. It was a bedroom, with a little bed all made up in pink and a dresser and a little school desk. On top of the dresser were candles and old photographs of a girl. I mean to say, she was a girl in some of them and a woman near as old as I was then in others. It was his sister, Finnerman's sister, the one what got run over by the car they never found. With the candles and all, the top of that dresser looked like a shrine, the kind of thing a decent home would have to the Virgin Mary. It made my skin crawl, thinking of Finnerman locked in there and those candles lit."

May's voice had grown hoarse. She paused again to soothe her throat with the uncut whiskey and resumed her story, hoarser still.

"While I was in there, I decided I'd have a poke around. I searched the dresser first and found her clothes, folded up just like she'd left them."

"She never lived in that house," Conneely said.

"Don't I know that?" May snapped. "He must have moved her things over, Finnerman, from the little house where they'd lived together. Moved them and kept them just so, God knows why. I searched the desk next and found school books and scads and scads of old movie magazines.

"I had one drawer left to search, the center drawer of the desk. Well, I'd had luck with desk drawers already that day, so I opened it up. Inside there was a little package wrapped in blue tissue paper. 'Here we go,' I thought, but there was nothing inside but a composition book, the kind I'd hated the sight of, when I'd been in school.

"Luckily, I thought to have a peek inside. I saw right away that it was a diary the dead girl had kept. She'd found a job, as I expect you know, with this American film company, and that was what this little book was all about: what actors she'd seen that day and what they'd said to her when she'd handed them their tea.

"I sat down on the edge of the little bed and began paging through the diary, forgetting all about Squire Finnerman and his silent, skulking ways. It was slow work, the writing all crabbled and me not the fastest reader, even of a fair hand. The first twenty pages or so were all sweetness and light. I grew sick of that soon enough and flipped ahead, thinking, 'Give us the dirt!'

"Then I saw some dirt, the littlest smudge of it. She was writing about the 'horrible thing that's happened,' and fretting over it, without saying what it was. I realized I'd flipped too far, that I'd skipped over the very thing I'd been looking for. I'd just started back, when I heard the sound of the front door closing right below me.

"I had that book in its tissue paper before I'd had the chance to feel fear, and the package back in its drawer. There was nothing for it then but to open that bedroom door and take my chances. I did it, expecting to see him there on the landing or coming up the stairs, his big hands knotted up in fists. But the landing and the stairs were empty. I closed up the room, blessing the softness of that lock. Then I hurried down those creaking stairs, my heart beating a hundred to the minute. I still had to do the hardest thing, you see, which was to put the key back where I'd found it.

"Finnerman was in his study, but not at his desk. He was pacing back and forth, still in his coat and hat, reading a letter. When he saw me in the doorway, he said, 'Yes?' I said, 'My duster, sir,' and pointed to his desk where I'd left it. He just nodded and went back to his reading. I made it to the desk without fainting dead, picked up the duster, and slipped the key—wet from my palm—into its drawer. Safe and safe."

Here May raised her glass again and found it had emptied itself. She pulled the bottle from her boot, recharged her glass, and then, in acknowledgment of the effect her storytelling had had, passed the bottle to Conneely. The guide drank gratefully and passed it on to Kerry, who also drank. Frank abstained, but

Danny did not, surprising even herself.

"I wasn't worried about getting another look at that diary," May said when the bottle was back in its boot. "Not now that I knew where the key was. I knew I'd have my chance that Friday night. Finnerman was a creature of habit. He always went to the graveyard to visit his sister and trim the grass around her stone before having his weekly pint at the local pub. One pint a week! An unnatural man, then and now.

"So I waited my chance, and I'm waiting still. For on that very Friday, Finnerman turned me from the house. Not for going into that locked room. He never suspected that, I'd swear an oath. No. He'd finally gotten around to noticing that a bit of his silver was missing. One place setting only from a service for twelve, property of a man whose table was never even set for two, not on Christmas itself.

"But that was the end of me and that diary. It's there to this day, unless the old leper's changed his spots. And I know he hasn't. For not six weeks ago, I saw him myself in the old graveyard, fussing about his sister's stone. He was true to his usual day, Friday, and his usual time, seven.

"Sixty years almost she's been in that ground, but to look at him sobbing there, you'd think the sod had just closed over her."

CHAPTER TWENTY-THREE

"Sweet secrets equal sweet tension."
—*Camelot Guide to Romance Writing*

"I tell you, people of business," May said after a suitable interval. "The morning's flying west, and I've much work to do, but I'll answer what questions you have. One from each of you, free of charge, as a courtesy. All others at one pound—euro, I mean—per question, in my hand."

She held out a broad flat palm. Danny noticed that it was unroughened and surprisingly clean. "You can be first," May said to Kerry, "since you paid for the story."

Kerry had his question on his lips. "You said that Finnerman only kept day workers in the sixties. He's an old man now and might need more help. Do you happen to know who he has around the place?"

Conneely and Danny looked at him sharply—the first in puzzlement and the second in alarm—but May only shook her head. "No one. Not a soul. Hasn't had for years. His money dried up on him around the time your other president, the actor fellow, was shot. He let his cook and his maid and his gardener go. The gardener was last, for Finnerman tried to keep up appearances for a time. Now his neighbor's sheep are his gardeners, and Finnerman gets paid for the grass they mow.

"Your turn," she said to Danny. "That dark look of yours is like a finger on my forehead. I'll not miss it when it's gone.

What's behind it now?"

Danny, embarrassed, took a moment to marshal her thoughts. They wouldn't marshal, so she snatched at the first one that passed. "That reference you found in the diary to the 'horrible thing,' what was the context? I mean, what was Bridey talking about in that entry?"

"You're right to ask me that. I should have said, for it was something that made my skin prick up that day and still does now. She was speaking of her soul, her 'immortal soul,' so she wrote. She was concerned for the souls of two others she didn't name over something they'd done. But her real worry was her own immortal soul. Was it in danger because she knew of this evil thing and said nothing? Should she speak to her priest of it? It nearly made me weep to think of the girl asking those questions, and her so close to her death.

"And speaking of questions," she continued, mastering her tenderer emotions, "those are your free ones. All others are a euro a toss. Pay me quick and ask them quicker. Your time is nearly run."

"I've not had my free question," Frank said quietly.

May froze for a second of her precious fleeting time. "You? I thought this was an American business deal. Sorry, lad. Ask me your question. But," she added, addressing Conneely, "this is the last free one. I'll not answer another, not if you were to get poor dead Gertie to rise up and bleat it."

Danny felt Frank put his hands on the back of her chair as he began. "You said you were planning to read the diary on a Friday when Finnerman went to visit his sister's grave, but you also told us you were a day worker. How could you hope to stay in the house after Finnerman had gone?"

"You may be more of a businessman than these Americans," May observed. "A lawyer, even. As to how I'd hoped to be left in the house when he'd gone, that was easy enough to work. I only had to start some big thing late in the day, something he couldn't stand to have unfinished until Monday. Taking all his good china out of its cupboard for washing, say. If he caught me trying that and stopped me in time, I'd just spill something, a pan of soapy water or a bucket of ashes, just as my day was ending. Then he'd make me stay and lock up after myself and think it served me right. But he'd on no account be late himself or miss going. Our trains would be the envy of the world if they were as regular as Seamus Finnerman was on that graveyard trip. Was and is to this day.

"And now your time is all used up. That extra free question did it. My generosity has cost us all dearly. But I'm a busy woman. Away with you now. This place would be a shambles if I did nothing but sit and gossip."

She might have gone on protesting, but Conneely was already herding his charges to the door and leading their chorus of thanks. He nearly had the thing done when Kerry escaped him, slipping back into the room and showering coins on the startled householder's lap.

"Does Finnerman keep a dog?" he asked, the tour guide's hand on his shoulder.

"A dog?" May spat again. "Why, the man's too cheap to keep mice."

It was a quiet car that drove north through a steady rain from Screeb, containing none of the wild speculating of the previous night's return from Galway. The instigator of that earlier speculation, Kerry, rode cross-armed in the backseat. He leaned forward but once, to ask Conneely if they had time to swing by White o' Morn.

"No. It's quite impossible. As I said, I'm not my own man this afternoon. Any other day, I'd say to hell with obligations. I've enjoyed your company that much. But not today. On no account. No."

There were sheep all about them: in the hilly fields on either side of the road and in the road itself occasionally, singly and in flocks. Brownish, wet sheep with a little spot of color on their sides, red or blue or yellow.

"Paint, of course," Conneely said, though no one had asked him. "To identify the owner. Like the branding in your western movies. What was that one with your friend Mr. Wayne that had so many cows in it? He was herding them to market, but some slip of a boy took them away from him."

"*Red River,*" Danny said. "Frank's a big fan of that one," she added, remembering their driver's angry reference to roping Maureen O'Hara. She hoped to produce a smile from Frank or at least to get him to turn his head, but he did neither thing.

"Ah yes, *Red River,*" Conneely repeated, rolling the R's. "A very dusty film. I remember thinking when I first saw it that it contained many parallels to the epic *The Cattle Raid of Cooley,* the Irish *Beowulf,* you know."

He began to name the parallels, the discourse taking them almost to the turn for Oughterard. Danny listened with one ear only. She was thinking of Bridey Finnerman's immortal soul and what might have imperiled it, and then of immortal souls in general, perhaps because the two words, "immortal" and "soul," fit so perfectly with the slow rhythm of the Ford's wipers.

Due to the literary lecture, Frank was forced to spot the last turn for home unaided. He was signaling for it when Conneely interrupted his summing up. "We'll go on a ways, Mr. O'Shea. Just a wee bit. Not as far as White o' Morn. I meant what I said about that discursion. But I feel I owe our patron something in compensation. There'll be a lane on your left with an old apple tree to mark it. We'll turn there."

Danny saw a turning, but Frank didn't slow for it, there being no tree nearby. They were almost upon it when Conneely grabbed his arm. "That's it, there. Brake, man. Yes, you have it, just mind the wall. Beg pardon for the excitement. The old tree must have died at last. Sad that."

They'd driven but a short way before he said, "There on the right. On that steep there."

Danny rolled down her window, both to improve her view and to escape Kerry, who was crowding her from the left.

On the hill was a large house, bleak and stark against the lowering sky. Though no light shone from its windows, Danny could make them out. Two especially drew her eye, two small windows above a little beak of a front porch.

"Yes," Conneely said, addressing their thoughts. "That's the very place. Seamus Finnerman's fine house. Or all that's left of it."

CHAPTER TWENTY-FOUR

*"Physical intimacy should heighten tension in your story, just
as it does in real life."*
—*Camelot Guide to Romance Writing*

They parted with Conneely at the same wet Oughterard corner
where they'd found him, the old man dismissing Kerry's offer
of a ride to his pressing appointment.

"I can't be seen with a car and a chauffeur," he said, "or all
my pub chits will come due at once. That would be the ruin of
me."

The remaining members of the party sought their lunch in
Doolin's, the cramped, smoky pub favored by the villagers in
which Kerry and Danny had first met Conneely. This was Kerry's inspiration.

"The food has to be good if the locals eat there," he said.
"It'll be like eating where the truck drivers eat in America."

"Are they known as dining authorities, your truck drivers?"
Frank asked as they worked themselves single file into the
crowded place.

"They're known as authorities on hemorrhoids and constipa-
tion," Danny informed him from her place at the end of their
line.

When they'd squeezed themselves around a table meant for
two, pipe smokers on either hand, Frank said, "Reminds me of

142

May O'Shaughnessy's," almost shouting it above the din of the place.

That din rendered normal speech quite useless and influenced the topic of their lunchtime conversation. Danny had expected it to consist of Bridey Finnerman's life and times, but Kerry refused to discuss the mystery at the top of his voice in so crowded and public a place. Instead, after they'd ordered their stew and bread and tea, he diverted them with the story of a cross-country trip he'd taken in eighteen-wheelers as research for an article on the truck-driving life.

"Jersey to Pittsburgh and back. Out on the Pennsylvania Turnpike, which was boring, and back home again on I-80, which was more boring and not as well paved. My first host's name was Alphonse, but he preferred his CB handle—his radio nickname, Frank—Wild Mouse."

"Did you have a handle yourself?" Frank asked.

"Of course: Wild Turkey. I didn't talk much on the radio, though; I mostly listened. It was the 'hot-enough-for-you?' level of discourse you hear in a saloon or a salon, only with static. But Alphonse ate it up. On the way home, I rode with a woman driver. Molly."

"And what was her handle?"

"Molly. Very straightforward lady. Unromantic, you'd say from just looking at her. Moe Howard haircut and overalls. But ten minutes east of Pittsburgh, she pulls out this book on tape. Jane Austen. *Persuasion.* By the time we crossed the Delaware River at the Water Gap, I was crying my eyes out."

"That reminds me, Danny. You ought to get your books put onto tape. You could read them yourself."

"God save the poor truck driver trying to navigate through those tears," Frank said, baiting her.

She didn't rise to it, tucking instead into her stew. "Last ladle of the pot," the waiter had told her as though handing her a prize. She found now that "last ladle of the pot" was Irish for gummy with little meat.

When she looked up from her bowl, she found that the bartender was staring at her. She vaguely remembered the overweight young man from her first visit to the pub, or at least remembered his professional attire: a red silk vest over a white T-shirt. The man held their eye contact for a long moment, and then looked away.

After lunch and the very brief drive home, Kerry announced that he would rest. What might be called the Conneely period of the trip had left him fatigued, he told Danny, though by his sister's reckoning, Kerry had done little but sit, either in boat or car or smoky farmhouse. Danny wanted to ask him if this fatigue was his illness catching up with him. She wanted to ask, too, about Kerry's parting question to May O'Shaughnessy, the one regarding Seamus Finnerman's dog. But Liddle's quiet central hallway, with Frank standing beside them, was no place nor time for either query.

The novelist considered a nap herself, considered it to the point of lying down on her bed. But she couldn't sleep. She slipped from the room and from the lodge, undetected by man and dog. It had occurred to her that her fey stalker, the girl in the brown coat, might approach her again if she made herself available. It would never happen if Frank were along for the walk; Danny was sure of that. This was an intuition backed up by an observation: The girl had avoided her in Cong because of Frank's presence.

So she walked along the lake on its stony strand. The mist-filled clouds had lifted themselves well off the earth at last. Though it was still overcast, the air was almost dry and certainly mild. Danny could see a fisherman or two on the water and, far ahead of her on the shoreline, a runner disappearing toward the horizon.

As she walked, Danny revisited their interview with May O'Shaughnessy. Unconsciously, she made a fictional scene of it, changing the setting from unpleasantly dingy to uncomfortably sinister and breaking up the old woman's long monologue with penetrating questions she hadn't thought to ask at the time. This reconstruction so occupied her that she failed to notice when the distant jogger turned about. By the time she did notice, the figure was close enough for Danny to decide it was a familiar one. A few strides later, she recognized Frank, and all thoughts of meeting her mystery woman flew from her head.

Running, Frank had a long, easy stride. Though she'd seen it only once before, on the road near Bunratty, Danny was sure she would have recognized that stride anywhere. He wore his old black sweats, the pants rolled up enough at the bottom to show a blaze of white sock above each very dirty shoe.

She thought for a second that Frank might wave and run past her and felt an identical second's unforeseen regret. But he pulled up easily and put his hands on his narrow hips. His skin was bright pink from his exertions and his hair damp.

"What were you smiling at just now?" he asked between breaths. "Was it my high-water pants? I'm trying to avoid the mud."

"I was just happy to see a friendly face."

He seemed to take the claim at something less than face value but replied, "Walk with me then while I cool down."

They took up the outbound course Danny had been following, discussing the topic denied them at lunch: the "horrible thing" from Bridey Finnerman's diary.

"So much for Kerry's bright idea that Bridey had been knocked up by one of the movie people," Frank said.

"That wasn't Kerry's idea. Conneely mentioned it last night

at the Abbey. Mentioned the talk of Bridey being pregnant when she died."

"Wherever the idea came from, the diary entry didn't bear it out. The horrible thing was something Bridey witnessed, not something she did herself. It may have been a man and a woman from the cast getting it on. Outside of the blessed bands of wedlock, for it to upset poor Bridey so."

"It might have been two men."

"Or two women. Could it have been anything but sex of some kind?"

"Nothing like sex for imperiling your immortal soul," Danny said and wished she hadn't. "Someone stealing from the company? Someone using drugs?"

"In 1951?" Frank asked. "And would Bridey have recognized a drug fiend if she saw one? Or two, rather, since the diary referred to a pair. The way May described Bridey's things, she didn't sound like a worldly girl."

"Sex it is then. From her movie magazines, Bridey would have known which stars were married and to whom. But would someone kill to keep an affair quiet?"

"I suppose you have to worry about that in your books," Frank said, kicking at one loose stone among the hundreds on the shore. "Selling the reader on a motive. Fictional people have to be well motivated to act. Logically motivated. Real people only have to be."

They walked on for a time, Danny marveling at how comfortable she'd become with this bare acquaintance. He, it turned out, was considering a problem. "There's something about this morning's business not sitting right with me."

"You mean, how did Conneely remember that the turn to Finnerman's was once marked by an apple tree?"

"What? No. I mean the questions that brother of yours chose to ask the O'Shaughnessy woman. About servants and dogs. Do you suppose he has a mind to read that diary himself?"

"I do," Danny said, feeling the joy and apprehension of a castaway who sees a strange footprint on her lonely beach. "Has he spoken of that?"

"He won't speak of it. Won't answer direct questions on the subject. Would he try something that foolish?"

"Sometimes I think that's what Furey means in Gaelic: doer of foolish things."

"Do you now? Do you mind if I test that? I've had it in my mind to for some time."

"What—" she started to say.

And then he was kissing her. Her mind had only a moment to protest professionally at this abrupt change of topic, at this unprepared-for twist, before she was kissing him back, pressing against him, and feeling the warmth of his run.

Then the mood was broken by a sound behind them, coming off the lough itself: the sound of something being dropped in an aluminum boat. They turned and saw a fishing boat containing a sheepish Cam Liddle, who waved to them, and a very sober Max Alnutt, who did not.

"What are the odds of that?" Frank asked.

CHAPTER TWENTY-FIVE

"Need to heighten sexual tension? Have one partner
throw it in reverse."
—*Camelot Guide to Romance Writing*

"Why not go for the diary? Don't you want to know the truth? And think of what it could mean to our book if we solve this thing. Tell me it wouldn't sell a few copies."

It was dinnertime. Nearly past dinnertime, though the Fureys had drunk far more than they'd eaten. They'd been forced from the lodge again, as Liddle's did not serve dinner this late in their season. The Fureys sat alone at a table in the tiny Oughterard restaurant with the long, consonant-bound name. Max had accompanied them but was currently standing near the dining room's piano, practicing his chitchat on the man at the keys. Frank had absented himself, ostensibly to write some letters. To Danny, this excuse would have been inadequate before their kiss on the shore. After it, it was inexplicable.

To distract herself from Frank's empty chair, Danny had had one more pint of stout than was wise. "Steal the diary," she said, just to hear the words. "Are you serious?"

Kerry's cards were on the table at last, revealed when the dinner dishes had been cleared and Max had stepped away. "Why not?" he asked and sipped his poteen, another of his special arrangements with management being in effect.

That management was represented in person by the man

who sat at the piano. This same young man, very tall and somewhat bent with it, had seated them and brought them their drinks. He'd later brought their food, perhaps after cooking it himself. Now he was joking with Max and picking at the piano's keys as though trying to recapture a barely remembered tune. Or so it seemed to Danny, who was close to remembering the tune herself under the powerful influence of the Guinness.

She tried to focus on Kerry's question: Why not? The obvious answers came easily. Stealing was wrong. Worse, it was illegal. They could go to jail. They could bring renewed pain and suffering to Seamus Finnerman, a soul who had done them no harm.

All excellent why-nots, but Danny chose to lead with a more metaphysical one: "We could lose the movie."

"*The Quiet Man?*"

"Yes. How would you like to think of a murder or some illicit affair every time you watch it?"

"It's too late to worry about that. And I don't mean that I don't have many viewings of *The Quiet Man* left. I have plenty. I mean we'll never watch it again without thinking of Bridey Finnerman. The movie's changed forever. We might as well know the truth."

"Then why don't we just ask him?"

"Who? Finnerman?"

"Yes. Drive out there, ring his bell, and ask him. We could pretend to be journalists. *I* could pretend to be a journalist. *You* could pretend to be a serious journalist. We're doing a story on *The Quiet Man*. We've heard about his sister. Or we could be even more honest and tell him we're writing a book."

"And he just spills his guts to us? The most secretive man in three counties?"

"Says May O'Shaughnessy." Danny would have spat if she'd had the gift. "But she keeps dead sheep. Why wouldn't he tell us? What's he got to lose now? The money stopped coming years ago. I'm surprised he hasn't sold his story long before this. Offer him something. A euro a question. Or ten."

"It's a thought," Kerry said, but absently.

Danny followed her brother's gaze to the restaurant's front window, hoping to see Frank. She saw a thin white nose against the dark glass and, behind it, Donal Conneely.

A moment later the old man was hanging his cap on one of their extra chairs and sitting himself in the other. "Back from the wars a little early," he said, "so I thought I'd ask how your afternoon had gone." He pointed to Danny's pint and then to himself, a signal to the man at the piano, who broke off his musical search on the very brink of success.

"What are we discussing in such loud voices?" Conneely asked.

"Burglary," Max said as he resumed his seat. "I could hear them over the piano. Kerry wants to rifle Bridey Finnerman's drawers."

He winked at Danny as he said it. He'd been winking or grinning at her all evening and generally being his charming best, which wasn't the reaction she'd expected to his witnessing Frank's kiss. Nor was Frank's reaction—making himself a void now filled by Conneely—what she had expected from him. She wondered briefly if Max had said something to Frank. Then she became conscious of Conneely's censorious eye, which was fixed not on Kerry but on herself.

The guide continued to study Danny all through the arrival of his pint, a noble one, despite the speed of its delivery. He sipped it appreciatively before asking her, "And what do you say to that?"

"I say it would be a lot more polite just to ask him to see it. The diary. Seamus Finnerman."

"Polite it would be," Conneely said. "But would it serve?

He's kept his secret for fifty years. The first twenty for filthy money and the last thirty for reasons of his own. It's surely occurred to him, a man with his business sense, that there's a windfall to be made from that diary. Yet he's never cashed the blank check. Why not?"

"The very question Danny was just asking," Kerry remarked.

"Was she? Well, it's an obvious one. And your sister's not a woman to overlook an obvious question. Surely the answer's just as plain: It can only be Finnerman's own guilt and shame holding him back. Guilt and shame over the use he made of his poor sister's death, the life he built upon it.

"That much we can fairly guess. But there may be more. He may have played some small part in that death. Maybe he knew what Bridey was about that last fateful night and failed to stop her. Maybe she'd confided in him, asked for his help, and he'd turned her away. Who knows?

"Whatever it is that's stayed Finnerman's hand since the mystery letters from America stopped coming, it can only have grown stronger with the passage of years. You'll have the devil's own time breaking its hold."

Danny, who had been expecting Conneely to second her caution, was confused into silence. Kerry was encouraged in direct proportion.

"Well said. Couldn't have done better myself, not without a word processor. Either of you spotted the men's room?"

He left the table in search of it, his bottle of poteen remaining behind to keep his place. There Donal Conneely's sharp eyes fell upon it and lit up as they did. In a flash, he'd emptied Danny's water glass into Kerry's and added two fingers of the clear liquor. Not to be outdone, Max drank off what remained of his own water and replaced it with the poteen, saying, "He hasn't given me a taste of this since Limerick."

"He'll never miss a wee dram," Conneely assured Danny,

who had witnessed the double theft dumbly.

Max and Conneely raised their glasses to one another in salute and knocked the drinks back. Danny watched their expressions change from eager anticipation to something like shock.

She laughed. "Too strong for you?"

"Strong enough," Conneely replied with the slightest shake of his white head.

The guide said no more until the poteen's owner reentered the dining room. Kerry paused at the piano to listen to a complete rendition of the mystery air, which the maitre d'– waiter–pianist had finally rediscovered.

His eyes on Kerry, Conneely recited softly, " 'His soul had approached where dwell the vast hosts of the dead.' "

"How do you know?" Danny whispered. She shot an accusing look at Max, who shook his head. "Did Kerry tell you that too?"

Conneely didn't hear the question, or ignored it. "That line is from a short story by Mr. James Joyce. 'The Dead.' It has a special connection to you and your brother, though I doubt you know what it is."

"Stephen Furey," Danny said promptly, for she was an English major, drunk or sober. "A character from 'The Dead.' Not really a character. A person one of the characters remembers. A guy this respectable married woman still pines for, long after his death."

"Very good. No doubt you've seen the movie version. For my part, I've read the story many times. Joyce and William Butler Yeats were the meat and drink of my generation, the way silly old movies seem to be for you and your Kerry.

"There's the decline of Western civilization for you, packed into a nutshell and tossed in your lap. My parents' generation had the Bible and Shakespeare as their common ground, the source of their imagery and allusion. We had Jimmy Joyce and Billy Yeats. You have moving pictures. And what will your children have? Bugs Bunny cartoons from the television, probably. How long till we're drawing on cave walls with burnt sticks again, I wonder?"

Kerry returned to the table then, but not to his seat. "Let's go, Danny. I'm shot."

"I'd advise coffee for your sister," Conneely said in a voice loud enough to place the order. "Unless you're doing the driving tonight."

"We walked," Kerry said.

"A wise precaution. Still, a little coffee will straighten the way home amazingly. Sit down while they make it, and let's discuss our next move."

"We're going to talk to Seamus Finnerman," Danny said.

"Of course, of course," the old man replied. "That's the obvious step. I only ask that you pause before you take it. Let me prepare the ground a bit, for one thing. Finnerman's not a man you can finagle with a bottle of whiskey. Not him.

"Then too, we need time to think out the best way to put the thing to him. I couldn't focus on my business this afternoon for worrying over that diary. If it's survived all these years and we do something that destroys it, it will be a tragedy. A fragment of history lost forever. Count upon it. If we should say the wrong word to Finnerman, that book will be on the peat and burning before his 'Go to hell!' stops ringing in our ears."

"How much of a pause are we talking about?" Kerry asked.

"One day only. I can't be with you tomorrow whatever you do. That's part of what I came to say tonight. Tomorrow's my big day of the month. I've a gaggle of Canadians lined up for a walking tour of Galway. Spanish Arch, Lynch's mansion, the whole shebang. My feet are aching just from thinking about it.

"But we can get together again on Saturday. Lunchtime

maybe. Compare our ideas, plan our campaign, and drive out to Finnerman's together. Tomorrow you could pass some other way. You could motor out to Leenane and look for the birthplace of your grandfather. What was it called again?"

"Letterfenny," Danny said, surprised that she hadn't thought of the place all day.

"Letterfenny, of course. Just the project for a sunny afternoon. Your feet will be as sore as mine by the time you find it, so we'll all be even. What do you say? Is it agreed?"

"Agreed," said Kerry readily.

"Sounds good," Max said.

Danny looked for quibbles and found none. "Agreed," she said.

CHAPTER TWENTY-SIX

"If you decide on a mystery plot, Part Two will contain the
nuts and bolts of the investigation."
—Camelot Guide to Romance Writing

Danny missed her quiet writing time by the lounge fire the next
morning, having overslept due to the extra pint from the night
before. She was doubly disappointed, as she'd also missed the
potential visit from Frank O'Shea, who had interrupted her
prior attempt to write in Liddle's lounge. She was anxious to
know how Frank felt, after a passage of time, about their kiss on
the stony shore of Lough Corrib. She was curious, as well, to
know why he'd been hiding himself away, almost from the moment of that kiss.

She was surprised to find her three companions all seated
and awaiting her in the sunlit breakfast room. Kerry was telling
an old story from his college days and Max and Frank were doing their best not to look at one another. Or so it seemed to
Danny from the coffee bar, where she'd stopped to overload a
cup of strong coffee with sugar. Then she took the open seat
next to Frank and across from Max, who smiled at her like he
had on their wedding day.

"Morning, Sis," Kerry said, abandoning his story in mid-
course. "You look like I feel. In fact, I'm not up for driving out
to Letterfenny today."

Danny had been preparing herself for some excuse from the

moment Conneely had suggested the trip. "Good," she said. "We can go and see Finnerman."

She was pleased to see Kerry discomforted for once.

"But we promised Donal we'd wait while he prepared the ground."

"He's only trying to get another day's wages out of you."

"How about we go and see May O'Shaughnessy again instead?" Kerry countered. "I'm pretty sure she knows more than she told us."

"I'm not going in that pigsty again."

"And I'm not going to Finnerman's."

Frank, attempting to broker a peace, said, "Letterfenny it is, then." And when both Fureys had glared at him, "Well, we've only the one car."

Max wiped his mouth with his napkin and tossed it on his plate. "I can fix that. Cam told me there's a rental agency at the hotel in the village. I'll hire a car for the day. I'll drive Danny over to talk to this Finnerman, and you two can go wherever you'd like."

Danny expected Frank to object to this distribution of passengers, and waited so long for him to do it that Max was up and away before she could speak herself. There was another chance when Max returned half an hour later with a tiny Audi. Danny was about to speak up when Frank intercepted her in the front lounge.

"It's best I stick with your brother," he said. "O'Shaughnessy will get his last penny if Max is the only one guarding him. I might even talk him into going to Aughnanure Castle, just down the Galway road, instead of out to Screeb. He's been talking of the visit you two made there ten years ago. You and Max have a nice drive. You could even go scouting out by Leenane if you finish with Finnerman early enough. For Letterfenny."

Danny couldn't read the Irishman's expression during this

very unsatisfactory speech. He'd delivered it to the lounge's current peat fire while poking at its flames, which were almost invisible in the bright sunlight Conneely had foretold.

"All right then," Danny said.

Frank and Kerry were still making their leisurely preparations when the novelist and her ex set out, heading west out of Oughterard. She could tell that Max was enjoying the Audi and its standard shift, which he worked up and down the gears more than was strictly necessary. Within a mile of Liddle's lane, she'd remembered how uncomfortable driving with Max could be, as he'd learned to brake with his left foot and often did it while his right was still pressing on the gas, forcing Danny first back in her seat and then forward against her belt in a rhythm only he could predict. Nor did he distract her with talk, only pointing now and again to a bit of scenery and whistling to himself.

He might have been remembering, as she was, their drives together across the Ohio countryside. Their weekend afternoons had often been spent in expeditions to little dots on the map rumored to have an antique shop or a restaurant of note. It was time spent together and yet not together, Danny now realized, with each traveling in a private bubble of unexpressed thought.

At Maam Cross, they turned right and began to look for the turn for Finnerman's road. Danny wasn't sure she'd find it, since she lacked both Conneely's aid and even the help of the landmark the old man had remembered, the apple tree, now gone. Nevertheless she spotted the turn in time for Max to downshift into it. At once she saw the house, gaunt and gray on its hilltop in spite of the sunlight.

Danny was tempted then to keep her promise to Conneely. She was sure that if Frank had been driving her, she would have given in to her sudden desire to be anywhere else. But she didn't care to shrink so in front of Max.

He pulled into the horseshoe drive that served the property, giving Danny her first close look at the house. The drive was paved in gravel, like May O'Shaughnessy's, and, like hers, it was being reclaimed by the surrounding lawn. The house served by the crescent was in better condition than Danny had expected, after her coaching on its dilapidation by O'Shaughnessy and Conneely, though not well kept, not by anyone's standards. The building's exterior surface, a stucco the color and consistency of grainy cement, was riddled with cracks still damp from yesterday's rain. The trim didn't lighten things, being dark blue, the paint peeling away from the windowsills and soffits. On the front door, where the color had been reapplied at some more recent date, it was merely mildewed. The little porch roof above the door, which Danny had seen as a beak when she'd first glimpsed the house, was missing a piece of its fancy rounded molding. It had been replaced by a flat board that kept out the weather but bespoke a despairing rearguard action.

The owl's eyes of O'Shaughnessy's vivid description, the paired windows directly above the front porch gable, stood in plain view, but Danny had only a second to take them in before Max was braking the car, left-footed, to a halt.

"Want me to do the talking?" he asked, grinning.

Danny was sorely tempted, knowing what she did about Max's powers of persuasion. But she held the temptation at a figurative arm's length. It was bad enough that she was grateful to have him along at that moment. Before Max could step clear of the car, she took the few steps to the mildewed front door and knocked. And knocked again. And no one answered.

"Out casting a line," Max suggested, his face turned toward the very blue sky.

He took a turn knocking, and then they gave up. As they drove down the crescent drive, Danny watched her mirror to see if a curtain moved in one of the widows behind them, but saw no sign of life.

At the end of the lane, Danny called for Max to stop the car, yanking on the emergency brake herself for emphasis. Their expedition to Finnerman's had accomplished nothing, but there was one small detail she could check. She circled the car and mounted the half wall of stone Conneely had warned Frank of during their original high-speed turn into the lane. There was no need to descend into the pasture beyond, for from her vantage point Danny saw what she was seeking. An old black stump.

So there had been an apple tree on that corner, or a tree anyway. That Conneely should have remembered it bothered Danny for no reason she could identify.

When she was back in the car, Max asked, "Left or right?"

She paused to consider. Left to Cong to try to find someone who remembered a hit-and-run from half a century before? Or right, to what? To Screeb, perhaps, and May O'Shaughnessy. Maybe it wasn't too late to rendezvous with Kerry and Frank.

"Right," Danny said.

Near Maam Cross her skin crawled with the now familiar feeling of another's eyes upon it. Always before the sensation had heralded an appearance by her mystery stalker, the young woman in brown. Danny looked about for her and saw instead a church.

She kicked herself mentally for not thinking sooner of a church, the surest source of genealogical information in Ireland. And this was Seamus Finnerman's own parish church, if he was Catholic, the ten to one bet. Bridey's, too, perhaps, depending upon how far Seamus's fine new house was from the one he'd shared with her. Even if he'd changed parishes, someone here might know the name of his former church, might know where his sister was buried.

"Pull in there," she instructed Max.

A small sign identified the church as St. Timothy's. It was a trim stone structure with a square bell tower supporting five steeples: a graceful slate-covered central one surrounded by four miniature copies in copper, one on each corner of the tower.

To the left of the church was a modest single-story house that was surely the rectory. To the right, a graveyard. So it was left or right again, and Danny paused to consider. She'd originally intended to ring the rectory bell, but now the feeling that they should start in the churchyard was so strong she recognized it as a hunch, a phenomenon she'd often encountered in fiction but seldom experienced.

The cemetery was framed by a fine mortared wall of the same stone as the church, its top edge as straight as any razor's. Compared with this perfection, the graveyard itself was a jumble, headstones everywhere, leaning every which way. Celtic crosses rose here and there above the confusion, the oldest and tallest so lichened over that they looked as though they'd been vandalized with white paint. All the older stones, large and small, were susceptible to this accretion. The newer ones were marble and immune. Some of the modern plots had been bordered with concrete curbing and covered over with marble chips, an arrangement that looked harsh to Danny's American eye but controlled the rampant grass.

"We're looking for Finnermans, I presume," Max said as they parted at the churchyard's gate.

Danny tried to be as methodical as the confusion of graves and pathways would allow. As a result, Max found the prize first: a tiny stone set right up against the back wall of the place. When Danny joined him there, she felt her breath catch in her throat. The first name on the stone was Bridget, the Christian name from which the nickname Bridey most likely derived. But the date beneath the name—the date of death only, in the Irish style, and half covered by grass—was January 19, 1958.

"It appears she lingered for a few years after that car ran her over," Max said.

"What the hell?" Danny asked in reply.

No one answered her.

Chapter Twenty-Seven

"Don't let your heroine shut down completely wondering if he'll call her again."
—*Camelot Guide to Romance Writing*

The rectory door was opened by the priest himself, Father Patrick Rich. "Rich in name and poor in ought else," he said as he ushered the Americans into his sitting room, a cluttered place overheated by its electric fire.

"You're too late for lunch and too early for tea, though I can offer you a cup as I always keep a kettle on. I never know who'll drop by."

The last words sounded a little plaintive to Danny, as though the real question wasn't who would drop by but whether anyone would at all. Father Rich was a spare man whose large thick-lensed glasses had an elegant golden bridge. His face was flat and very smooth, as though worn away by water. Danny guessed him to be nearing sixty, based on the worn face and on his hair. It was brown with the faintest trace of Frank's red and it lay in an early Beatles swoop across the priest's forehead.

"Tea would be great," Max said for them, as Danny was busy wondering if the priest's dated hairstyle was indeed a tribute to the Fab Four or Herman's Hermits or merely to his own lost youth. After Rich left them in the much-doilyed front room, she examined photographs of what she took to be his extended family. None were very new, she noted, and all were softly focused.

"I saw you out among the graves earlier and thought you might stop in," Rich said when he came back, clattering tray in his hand. "Looking for a relative, were you?" Like his face, the priest's voice was worn, and Danny felt herself leaning forward in her chair to hear him as he prattled on. "You're Americans, as I couldn't help noticing. Your clothes and all; I can always pick you out. After your roots, are you?"

"Not today," Danny said. "We're interested in a woman buried out there. Bridget Finnerman."

"Bridey?" the priest asked promptly.

Danny nearly dropped her tea. "You knew her?" she asked before she'd done the math. Rich could barely have been ten when the woman he'd named so familiarly died.

Luckily, he didn't take offense. "I? No. I'm not as ancient as all that. She passed away a long time before I came to the parish. But I've heard her story, the poor soul." Here the priest hesitated and, Danny thought, changed his direction slightly. "And of course I know her brother."

"Seamus," Danny said.

"Yes, that's right. Seamus Finnerman. Do you know him yourself then?"

The novelist shook her head very casually. "You mentioned Bridey's story."

"The story of her sad death," Father Rich explained. "Not her life before. She died too young to have much of a life, I'm afraid."

"How did she die?"

"In a traffic accident. She was struck and killed in a lonely stretch of road."

"Near Cong."

"Cong? No. The other way entirely. Just south of here and a

163

little west. At night it was, a foggy night. No one knows why she was out or where she was going. Two of the mysteries about the business. A lorry—a truck, you know—ran her down. The driver—his name was McFall if I'm remembering right—was found to have been drinking."

"What were the other mysteries about her death?"

The priest waved a hand. "Nothing really. We shouldn't gossip."

Hating herself as she did it, Danny nudged Max with her elbow and went through the motions of preparing to leave, setting her teacup down and saying, "We're taking up too much of your time."

Max, always a quick study, reached for his windbreaker, adding, "You're a busy man."

As Danny had expected, Rich reacted with signs of panic. "Not at all. I'm happy to tell you what I know. Please keep your seats. Would you like another cup of tea? A biscuit? It's just that some of the mysteries I mentioned—shouldn't have mentioned but did—are just idle speculation. There was talk, I think, that the girl's death might not have been an accident. That it might even have been suicide. My predecessor, Father O'Higgins, wouldn't let a word of that be spoken in his hearing. He wanted Bridey to be buried in consecrated ground, and of course she couldn't have been if she'd taken her own life."

Father Rich's slightly magnified eyes ceased to focus on his guests or on anything else in the room. He held his teacup up to his chin and spoke across it, musingly. "Father O'Higgins was a sentimental man. Too sentimental really. He baptized Bridey, you know, and gave her her First Communion. It was very important to him that he bury her, too. But the truth of a thing is always more important, far more important, than the forms and rituals. If Bridey had taken her own life, being buried in blessed earth wouldn't make her lie easier. It might even

164

disturb her rest."

Danny noted the oddness of this last remark, but only just. She was preoccupied with working up her nerve to ask a hard question. "Was there any talk that Bridey might have been pregnant?"

"That talk especially Father O'Higgins wouldn't tolerate. He couldn't, could he? It supported the idea that she'd taken her own life by giving her a reason to do it. And it cast the darker shadow of murder on her, since she would have taken her child's life with her own."

They sat for a time with only the hum of the fire and the ticking of a mantel clock to fill the silence. Though confused by the information they'd been given, Danny was impressed by the quantity of it. So impressed in fact that she became distrustful of the source.

"Bridey died in 1958, according to the stone," she said.

"Fifty years ago," the priest observed. "My my."

"How long have you been here at St. Timothy's?"

"Twenty-odd years, though it's hard to believe. I came here in 1984."

"And you heard Bridey's story soon afterward?"

"I suppose."

"How is it you remember it so clearly after twenty years?"

Again the priest hesitated, and again Danny had the sense that he'd begun to make one answer and then switched to another. "It's still spoken of from time to time. You know how we Irish are with our stories. But I should ask you, what's your interest in Bridey Finnerman?"

The priest's mention of stories had suggested the way to take, and Danny took it. "I'm a writer. Someone told me that Bridey's history might make a good book."

"But who would know the ending of it?" Father Rich asked his teacup.

CHAPTER TWENTY-EIGHT

"Make the ex-who-won't-go-away your go-to play."
—*Camelot Guide to Romance Writing*

Danny and Max stayed with the priest long enough to repay him for his confidences. When they said good-bye at last and regained the Ford, it was midafternoon. Danny had already abandoned her plan to revisit May O'Shaughnessy, abandoned it back in the rectory sitting room while pretending to listen to a long explanation of hurling. She had no need now to cross-examine the old woman. She was confident that O'Shaughnessy had lied to them about the contents of Bridey's diary. Perhaps about everything.

She spoke this conclusion aloud to Max, and he came up with its corollary: "If the old lady lied to you, so did Donal Conneely. We'd better tell Kerry before he adopts the guy."

On the drive back to Liddle's, Danny tried to recall the complete history of their relationship with the tour guide, from the evening they'd met him in Doolin's until their parting on an Oughterard street corner late Friday night. Over and over the American relived it, looking for some explanation of the wide gap between Conneely's story and Father Rich's.

They reached the real Oughterard before she'd found one. There she espied the real Doolin's and fired off another of her precipitate orders: "Grab that parking space across from the pub!"

Max did so, and Danny hurried him across the busy street, drawn by a hunch as strong or stronger than the one that had led them into the graveyard at St. Tim's.

The little pub was busy, if not quite as crowded as it had been when she and Kerry and Frank had lunched there on gummy stew. While scanning the room, Danny spotted the heavyset bartender in the red vest, and she realized at once what had brought her there. It was a memory of the look that same bartender had given her the day before, the very freighted look that had never been explained. It was a loose end that Danny determined to tie up.

They squeezed in at the bar, and the young man came over, pushing a damp towel before him. He'd taken the Americans' order and was reaching for a glass before the look of recognition came into his dark, almost black eyes.

"Right," Danny said, nodding. "Me again. Have one with us?"

The bartender nodded back, poured Danny's ginger ale on the rocks and drew pints for himself and Max. At this close range Danny could see that the man had peculiarly dark hair for an Irishman. It curled on his head, matted his forearms, and peppered his heavy jaw.

"I was in for lunch yesterday," Danny began. She sipped her drink for inspiration. "You looked like you had something you wanted to tell me."

"T'was nothing really," the other said and sipped his stout, perhaps for his own inspiration. "I waited on you the other night when you were here with the other American. You were talking with the Don."

"Donal Conneely."

"Aye. You've seen him since?"

"Yes," Danny said. "Why?"

"Just a friendly word then. Keep your wits about you with

that one. And your hand on your wallet."

"What are you saying?"

As he turned to go, red vest laid a broad finger beside a broader nose. "Just a friendly word, as I said. We don't want anyone's vacation ruined, now do we? Not in Doolin's."

"Now he warns us," Max said.

"Someone else did, too," Danny said. "I mean, someone else gave me the same kind of look."

One just as dark, she thought. *Dark.*

That word brought it back. She remembered the sleek clerk behind the high-altar desk in the Ashford Castle Hotel, whose hair was as dark as red vest's. As dark as a raven's wing, Conneely had phrased it. The clerk had given their party a hard examination, which Conneely had explained away. Just the animosity the hotel staff would naturally feel for a gypsy tour guide, he'd said, but had it been?

"I need a phone," Danny said, looking around.

"We're parked in front of a drugstore."

They found a phone there, along with a team of helpful locals to instruct them in its clicks and beeps. With their aid, Danny reached an operator who connected her to the Ashford Castle Hotel.

A woman answered. Danny asked to speak to the desk clerk who'd been on duty Thursday morning, describing him, in her excitement, as "the guy who looks like a black cat with a winter's worth of canaries stashed away."

The woman laughed, collected herself, and said, "That would be Mr. Neville. One moment please."

The phone began to beep a warning, and Danny hastily inserted all the change she had left. As the last coin dropped, a slightly nasal voice on the other end of the line said, "This is Mr. Neville."

Danny unconsciously matched his clipped tones. "My name's

Furey. My brother and I visited your hotel Thursday morning with a friend and a tour guide named Donal Conneely. We had another guy with us, first name Jeffrey, who claimed to be a long-time employee of the hotel. Do you remember seeing us?"

"I might," Neville said. "What is this regarding?"

"A look you gave us. I have reason to believe it might have been a warning look. Was it? And did it involve Donal Conneely?"

There was a pause. "Tell me, Ms. Furey, are you a guest of the Ashford Castle?"

"No," Danny said.

"Have you ever been?"

"No."

"Then I'm afraid it would be inappropriate for me to say anything more to you."

"Good day" was surely next.

"Mr. Conneely put a financial proposition to my brother and me the day we visited the hotel. We're thinking of investing with him. If it should turn sour and become a police matter, your hotel will be mentioned in the investigation. You'll probably be called to testify yourself."

Another pause. Then a grudging answer: "I shouldn't give Mr. Conneely any money if I were you."

"Why not, Mr. Neville?"

"Just my considered judgment."

"Sorry. The deal's too good to pass up without more reason than that. I guess we'll go ahead with it."

A third pause, briefer than the first two. "Suppose for argument's sake there were a file maintained by a hotel, a file of confidence men who prey on tourists. And suppose Mr. Conneely's photo and history were in such a file."

"Any chance of a tourist seeing the file, assuming it existed?"

"None whatsoever."

"Okay. How about answering a more straightforward question? The man with Conneely on Thursday, the one in the pink blazer who called himself Jeffrey. Was he ever an employee of the hotel?"

"No."

"No period or not as far as you know?"

"No period," Neville said, his impatience sounding a warning in Danny's ear like the pay phone's earlier beeping. Time was running out, and there was something she needed to double-check.

"Just one more thing. Have you ever heard the story of a young girl who was killed in a hit-and-run accident near the hotel back in 1951 while *The Quiet Man* cast was staying there? Her name was Bridey Finnerman."

"Certainly not."

"You've never heard the name Bridey Finnerman?"

"No period," Neville said, showing a flash of wit. "Now good day."

CHAPTER TWENTY-NINE

"All men are liars. Make it work for you."
—Camelot Guide to Romance Writing

As the little tin bell on the chemist shop's door tinkled its good-bye behind them, Max said, "You're on a roll, short stuff."

Only a day ago, his use of his old nickname for Danny would have earned him a sharp rebuke, but now it passed all but un-noticed. Danny was thinking again of what turn in the road to take. Max summed up the options as though reading her thoughts, something else that would have irritated her in a less preoccupied moment.

"Do we talk to your brother or the police?"

"Kerry first," Danny said.

They looked for the familiar Ford in Liddle's lot, but it wasn't there. Max pulled up perpendicular to the lodge's front door.

"I'll drop you here," he said. "I might as well turn the car in before the rental kid leaves for the day. I can walk back. It was nice spending some time together."

"Yes," Danny said. Max seemed to expect her to say more. Her impulse was to add that their quiet afternoons together had been among the many things Max had given up when he'd decided to sleep with Lola. But pointing that out would have been a churlish way to repay him for his company, so she said, "I was sorry to hear that you and Lola had broken up."

"Biggest mistake of my life," Max said.

Danny was out of the Audi before she'd tried to parse that sentence. Did he mean that breaking up with Lola had been the biggest mistake of his life? Or that Lola had been?

She was still chewing on it as she passed the communal lounge, empty even of dogs. Mrs. Liddle caught her just beyond it. She called to Danny from the open office with a phone in her hand.

"A call from America for Mr. Alnutt," the landlady said. "Some sort of emergency." She handed over the phone and bustled out.

Danny decided that something had happened to Lola and immediately regretted the hard thoughts she'd just had of her onetime friend. But the caller was Lola herself.

"Danielle," she said. "It's good to hear your voice. I guess I have to call a foreign country to talk to you these days."

"What's the emergency? Is it Max's mom?"

"What? No. I just said that to get a little service. The gal that answered only wanted to take a message, and Max hasn't been returning my calls. So, is everything okay? Are you having a great time? Sorry to hear that your brother's sick. Has the shopping been good?"

"Thanks," Danny said on Kerry's behalf. "I haven't done any shopping."

"That's what you get for being over there with two guys. If I'd come along like I wanted, we'd have hit all the shops."

Danny, who'd been watching the hallway for a glimpse of Kerry or Frank, now turned her back on the door and gave her full attention to the phone. "You and Max were together when Kerry called?"

"You almost can't get more together. We were in bed. I told Max to call back and get a ticket for me, but he said it would be counterproductive."

"Why?"

"He didn't think me being around would set the right mood. He's talked to you about the money, right?"

"No."

Lola sighed. "I knew he wouldn't. Listen, when your brother called about this Ireland getaway, we decided it would be the perfect time to ask you about a loan. We're in a little bit of a money crunch at the moment. Since you're doing so well and since you walked away from the marriage with half of Max's savings, I thought you wouldn't mind helping us out."

Danny found herself slowly counting to ten, like a character in a sitcom. "I'll definitely talk to Max about that," she said.

"Great. Well, we'll need another loan to pay for this call if I stay on much longer. Thanks for your help."

"No, thank you," Danny said and hung up.

Just outside the office door she literally bumped into Frank. He was coming from the bedroom wing, and Danny wondered at his getting in from the lot without her noticing. This while he was holding her at arm's length, examining her.

"I'll say this for Mr. Alnutt; he always does your color good."

"Mrs. Alnutt the second in this case," Danny replied, the sight of Frank easing her gritted teeth. "Where's Kerry?"

"Lying down. The drive to Screeb and back winded him, so he said."

"You talked to May?"

"We did not. She wasn't home. And Mr. Finnerman?"

"Also not home. But we made progress." She started to lead him to the lounge and changed her mind. Max would be back at any moment, and she didn't want Frank to witness that conversation. She headed for her room instead, Frank at her heels. At her doorway, he hesitated.

"What will Mrs. Liddle think?" he asked.

"If Kerry's asleep," Danny said, "I don't want to wake him."

They made it inside the room without Mrs. Liddle noticing,

but Frank did not relax. In fact, he grew more awkward, reminding Danny inevitably of the moment on the shingle when Max and Cam Liddle had caught them in an embrace.

"There's something I have to tell you," he said.

"Me first," Danny said. Ever since she'd left the chemist's in Oughterard, she'd been feeling the storyteller's tug-of-war, the conflict between holding one's story and giving it away. But, like any true storyteller, she could hold out only so long.

"This is important," Frank said.

Danny saw in his azure blue eyes that it was, so she gave up her rightful place in the queue and waited.

After a full minute, Frank said, "You go ahead."

It spilled out of her then, the finding of Bridey Finnerman's grave, the talk with Father Rich, and the warnings she'd wheedled out of the barman and the hotel clerk regarding Conneely. Frank's countenance, grim at the start, was grimmer by far at the finish.

He took her hand. "Kerry shouldn't be sleeping through this."

They crossed the hall to the men's communal room and found it empty. Danny felt a chill wind pass through her.

"When did you get back from Screeb?"

"An hour or more ago. Why?"

So she hadn't missed their return while on the phone. "The car was gone when we got back fifteen minutes ago."

Frank patted his pockets and searched the nearest dresser top. "The keys are gone."

CHAPTER THIRTY

*"Impossible challenge number one: Make your climactic scenes
inevitable and totally unexpected."*
—*Camelot Guide to Romance Writing*

"He's gone to Finnerman's house," Danny said. "He's going to
steal the diary."

Frank made a sound like a growl in his frustration and pushed
past her out the door. "Your brother. He could talk about nothing else but Finnerman's yesterday. Today he wouldn't mention
it, the sly one. Him and his naps."

In the parking lot, they confirmed what Danny had said, the
Ford was gone. Frank consulted his watch.

"Almost six. Finnerman will be leaving for his sister's grave
soon."

Help came then from an unexpected source. Max Alnutt
pulled into the lot in the little Audi. "Friday's the same here as
home," he said. "The rental clerk left early. I waited around for
one pint and then gave up."

Danny and Frank were in the car almost before its driver's
explanation was over. Their own explanation, given after Danny
had ordered Max back onto the road, lasted them through the
village.

"Maybe Finnerman won't be there," Danny said sometime
later. "Maybe he's in a nursing home or on vacation. Maybe he
really does tend Bridey's grave on Friday evenings."

Max crushed that last hope as they swayed together for the Maam Cross turn. "Don't you remember how long the grass was around her stone? Nobody's been there this month."

They'd no sooner made the sharp left onto Finnerman's lane than they saw the red Ford standing in the tall weeds that had grown up to fill a gap in the border wall. Max slowed to a crawl to pass the car safely in the narrowed space.

Frank, leaning out his open window, said, "Empty. And parked facing the house. So much for a quick getaway."

Danny barely heard this complaint regarding Kerry's burglary technique, she was that overtaken by the reality of the thing. Max accelerated dangerously, then braked more so to make the turn into the horseshoe drive. They had no thought of hiding the car or of stealing up unheard. Only of getting there in time.

Max parked hard on the front steps, and Danny was out and climbing them without waiting for the others. She had her hand out, reaching for an old black knocker, when she noticed that the door was ajar. By then Frank was at her shoulder, whispering: "He's finagled the lock. He's inside."

Danny pushed the door open, and the low evening sun lit a large empty space, a front hall. "Mr. Finnerman!" she called out. Then, less boldly, "Kerry?"

They were listening carefully, standing perfectly still, Frank's hand squeezing Danny's shoulder, or else they would have missed the faint reply. "Upstairs, Sis."

They crossed the bare hall and mounted the steps, Danny leading and certain of their destination: the secret room. As they ascended, their eyes adjusted themselves to the gloom, first of a landing that reversed the direction of the stairway, then, after a further short climb, of an upper hallway. They were facing the front of the house then and a room directly above the entryway. May O'Shaughnessy's famous locked room. Only its door was not locked nor even closed. The rescuers approached it circumspectly, for they could see two men within the room, and one of them was armed.

This they saw by the evening glow coming in through the owl-eye windows: Kerry and an old giant of a man—white-haired and white-browed with heavy jowls and a huge beak of a nose as pale as bone—sitting almost knee to knee. The bent giant held a fowling piece whose barrels were pointing in Kerry's general direction, if not quite at the man himself. Only when the newcomers had crept to the very threshold did Danny note that the room was far smaller than she'd envisioned and not a dead girl's bedroom or anyone else's. It was an ordinary bathroom, not very modern and not overly clean. The old man was seated on the edge of a bathtub and Kerry on the closed lid of a toilet.

"Mr. Finnerman snuck up on me as soon as I got in here," Kerry said, nodding toward his captor. "I thought I'd have a heart attack. Then he did have some kind of attack. I've been afraid to leave him."

Danny knelt beside Finnerman, more frightened by the blue color of the man's pendulous lower lip than by his gun. Nevertheless, she placed a hand on the twin barrels as she whispered in his ear, "My brother means you no harm. He was tricked into coming here." And then, to make the claim more probable, "We're Americans."

Finnerman blinked twice, once in slow motion and once at normal speed. "Americans, are you? And tricked, you say? You must tell me the story."

His hands dropped away from the gun, and Danny took up its weight, passing it to Kerry, who stood the thing carefully in the corner behind him, where it made an odd trio with a scouring wand and a plunger.

"Help me down to my study," Finnerman said, starting to rise.

"We have to call for a doctor," Danny protested.

"We can call from there."

They moved in a slow procession, Danny in the lead and switching on whatever lights she could find, Frank and Kerry supporting Finnerman's weight between them. The would-be cat burglar was only a little steadier than his intended victim, and he passed his job to Max, who had been awaiting them on the landing.

By then Danny had found and illuminated the study, a room whose odor was pipe tobacco and whose interior decoration was as dedicated to golfing as that of Liddle's lounge was to fishing. She poured Finnerman a glass of water from a carafe on a well-appointed bar, handing it to him after the men had sat him in a much settled easy chair near a cold fireplace.

"Bless you, my girl," he said when he'd drained it. "It's my heart, you know. Weak forever and ever. Brandy now, if you please. About half that much. And help yourselves to some."

Frank served him while Danny phoned the doctor, using a number Finnerman rattled off from memory. A service answered in the professional's place. Danny asked that an ambulance be sent and rang off. "We should move our cars."

"I'll do it," Max said, collecting keys from Kerry, who was slumped in an easy chair of his own.

Frank was attempting to light a fire under the supervision of Finnerman, who had been much restored by his brandy. Danny moved a footstool to the arm of the old man's chair and sat down.

"A tour guide named Donal Conneely told us a story about your sister," she said when she'd gotten Finnerman's attention. "He told us she'd worked for a movie company and that she'd been hit by a car and killed in 1951."

It was a very short retelling of Conneely's tale, but there was time enough for Finnerman's large face to assume a look of total confusion, for the shaggy brow to rise up and the hooded eyes to show their mottled whites. "He said that, this Conneely?"

"Yes," Danny said, her hand on the rough tweed of Finnerman's sleeve. "You did have a sister named Bridey, didn't you?"

"I did."

"But she died in 1958, not 1951, didn't she?"

"January 19, 1958," the old man said, nodding.

"And Bridey never had anything to do with the movies, did she?"

"Never in life. But you've not told me why you came. Was it because of Bridey?"

"Yes. Conneely told us that she'd been murdered, maybe by an American, and that there was a clue to it hidden in this house."

"In my bath?" Finnerman asked, his brows ascending even higher.

From the depths of his chair, Kerry laughed to himself and at himself.

Danny said, "In a locked room above your front door. It was something Conneely made up, like the rest of his story." Kerry looked up at this finally, but said nothing. "You don't know him, Donal Conneely?"

"No."

"Then you don't know why he'd weave his story around your sister's death?"

"His murder story? It could have been because Bridey was murdered herself."

"Who by?"

"Me," her brother said.

CHAPTER THIRTY-ONE

"Every character should have a story to tell."
—*Camelot Guide to Romance Writing*

"Oh yes," Finnerman said. His voice was so like a rumble coming up from the earth below them that Danny was sure she could feel it through the soles of her shoes. "I caused my Bridey's death, though I never meant her as much as a single raindrop's harm. It was my fault she was out on the road that night. My fault that the truck ran her down."

"Truck?" Kerry asked, catching his sister's eye again. Danny said nothing, and the only answer Finnerman made was to hold out his empty glass.

"I'll have another, I think," the old man said. "You'll join me, won't you? We'll drink to her." Frank refilled his host's glass. He'd already given Kerry a brandy, poured at Finnerman's first invitation but so far untouched. He now poured one for himself and handed another to Danny.

"To my sister."

They all drank, the Fureys never taking their eyes from one another. Then Finnerman began.

"Forty years ago and more—can it be so long?—I stood in the way of Bridey's happiness. She was in love with a local gadabout named Robart. Michael Robart. But he was so much older and with such a wild reputation and Bridey so young and delicate, only a girl in school, that I'd hear nothing of it. I was

Bridey's whole family and her guardian, though I was still a young man myself.

"The way she went on. She'd die, she said, if she couldn't have her Michael, her handsome one. No evil word about him was true. No thought of her future would sway her. But I was just as adamant. And so we went back and forth until we came to this agreement: She would finish school—a boarding school in Galway, the best I could afford—then, if she still wanted Robart, I'd give them my blessing.

"We'd no sooner struck the bargain than I started in to break my part of it. I went to Robart and said to him, 'End it with my sister and I'll pay your passage to America.' Things were bad here for a young man then, and as many as could were going elsewhere. I didn't have much money, but Robart had none. And I'd heard he was a man who'd be blinded by the littlest glint of it. Sure enough, he was. He gave over Bridey, that treasure, and shook my hand on the deal.

"Shortly after that her heart was broken and shortly after that she died."

A healthier color had come into Finnerman's face. Danny was heartened enough by it to ask, "You think she might have taken her own life?"

"Or been made careless by her despair. She had no reason to be wandering in the dark that night but despair. Aimless, heedless despair."

Here Finnerman looked around the slowly darkening den, moist-eyed and trembling. Then Max reentered the room, moving silently, but bringing the old man back to them.

"What happened to Robart?" Danny asked.

"He went away after Bridey died. That was one bargain I kept. I paid him his money, though neither of us could look the other in the eye as I counted it out. Then he went to America. He's still there, and still hating me, if he's breathing. And I don't blame him, given what I did to him.

"His passage money came from her insurance, Bridey's. So did this house, come to that. I should have given the money to the poor. Robart thought it was cursed, and well he might have, since it had cost him so much. Since my folly had cost us both so much.

"But I did far worse to Bridey, my own sister. I denied her her only chance for love, which is another way of saying I denied her her life. As short as her time on earth was, it would have been complete if I'd only let her have her Michael. She might have had something before she died that some people never find, though they live to be ninety."

He broke off then, shaking his head and, after a moment, sobbing.

Danny, thinking of the fine empty house Finnerman had bought with his sister's settlement, a prison, as the American saw it, for a single inmate, wondered whom the tears were for.

They stayed with Finnerman until the ambulance arrived. In the bustle that followed, Kerry and Frank and Max slipped out of the house. Danny would have, too, but while crossing the barren front hall she'd spotted the entryway to a parlor. By the hall light, she could make out the shapes of furniture and, on a mantle, the frames of photographs.

She stepped inside the room and switched on a table lamp. Half a dozen photographs sprang to life in the mantle grouping. One was an antique wedding photo, the groom seated, the bride standing behind him. Finnerman's parents, or perhaps his grandparents. There was a picture of Finnerman as a boy of ten or so with a baby—his sister—in his arms, and another of him as a young man, thin and straight. Next to it was the photo Danny had been looking for.

She took it down from its place and carried it to the light. The black-and-white portrait, a school photo surely, showed a girl of about sixteen with large dark eyes and an open lovely smile.

Danny had never seen the smile, but she recognized the face. As she'd feared for some time, as she'd known without admitting to herself that she knew since her first visit to St. Timothy's churchyard, the young woman in the photograph was the one who had dogged her steps all week, the woman of the brown coat and blue scarf.

"Bridey," she said aloud.

CHAPTER THIRTY-TWO

"You set the table in Part Two. In Part Three, kick it over."
—Camelot Guide to Romance Writing

There could be no summing up or comparing of notes on the drive home, divided as they were between two speeding cars. Max again drove the Audi, with Kerry as his passenger. Frank and Danny followed, the latter dividing her attention between the Audi's tiny taillights and the sides of the road, which she scanned for a figure in brown.

To distract herself from this, she said, "Earlier this evening you started to tell me something. Now would be a good time."

"It would not," Frank said. "You've enough on your mind already."

During a brief polling in Oughterard, they determined that no one was in the mood to eat, so they returned to the lodge. There they found that the lounge—their lounge—had been taken over by a party of German fishermen, lately arrived. The Americans repaired instead to Danny's room for their conference. For seats, each selected a bed from the room's foursome of beds, which were arranged in a disjointed rectangle. The drivers, Max and Frank, lay back wearily on their respective couches. Kerry, across from Danny, settled lightly on his.

"Like I told Max," he said, taking up a pillow from the bed and holding it in his lap, "I was up in that damn bathroom before I suspected we'd been lied to. Up to the door of it

184

anyway, which wasn't locked as it should have been. What tipped you off?" This to his sister. "The apple tree?"

It was as good a place to start as any, Danny thought, a concrete suspicion to stand as a symbol for all the vague ones she'd been feeling. She repeated the story she'd earlier told Frank, though without the same enthusiasm. She'd outsmarted Kerry as well as Conneely and should have reveled in that, but somehow she couldn't.

As she summarized the chat with Father Rich, Danny remembered the priest's odd pauses and changes of tack and reconsidered them in the context of the photograph she'd seen of Bridey and the knowledge that she'd seen the woman herself again and again that week. Had the lonely priest seen the dead girl, too, glimpsed her from time to time through his rectory window, standing at her untended grave? Was that the real reason her story had been so fresh for him?

None of this internal wandering was mentioned to the others, Danny being unready to admit that she'd been visited by a ghost, but it led to odd gaps and pauses in the novelist's own storytelling. When Kerry prompted her for the third time, Danny moved to more solid ground, her interview with the barman at Doolin's and her call to the Ashford Castle Hotel.

"Donal a con man," Kerry said. "How'd we miss that? It's so damn clear in retrospect. All that business about Finnerman visiting his sister's grave every Friday. He laid that on with a trowel, didn't he? Him and his unimpeachable source May O'Shaughnessy. Then he carefully set our showdown with Finnerman for Saturday. So we'd have to act fast if we wanted to steal a look at that diary or hang around for a week until the coast was clear again. I walked right into that one."

"Ran in," Danny said, but not harshly. She roused herself long enough to move to Kerry's side and feel his brow. It was cooler, she suspected, than her own.

Their conference room was lit by a single lamp, one that stood on the lowest of the mismatched dressers. As Danny settled herself again, she spied an object beneath this lamp. It was a little blue booklet, opened slightly so it would stand up on its own. Her passport. Despite the advice of guidebooks, Danny seldom carried it when she went about, preferring to hide it in her room. The maid must have found it, she decided, and stood it there so Danny couldn't miss it.

Kerry broke into her thoughts with a question. "So what's Conneely been after? It can't have been the money I've been paying him. He knows enough about *The Quiet Man* to have earned that without all the lying."

"He knows an awful lot about Bridey Finnerman as well," Frank said. "But I can't understand why he used her in his made-up story. I mean, why use a real girl whose stone we could find and whose story we could check? Why not just make up some name? And why point us toward a real brother with a real house?"

"So a real idiot, me, would break into that house," Kerry said.

"But why?" Frank insisted. He asked the question of Danny, but she'd come to the end of her answers.

"I expected Finnerman to clear all that up tonight," she said. "I was sure he could. But he'd never heard of Conneely."

"Don't put yourself down, Sis. You solved most of it. I was the one who swallowed the hook. Damn. We got off too easy. I got off too easy. What if Finnerman had died? What if he still does?"

"What if he'd shot you?" Max asked without opening his eyes. "Would your conscience be clearer then?"

Danny absented herself from this discussion, using as her excuse the passport she'd spotted earlier on the dresser. As she crossed the room to it, she thought again how odd it was that the passport should have been propped there like a tiny wine list. She was sure she could remember slipping it under her dwindling supply of clean underwear. Opening the drawer where those delicates resided, she found them in elaborate disarray. She opened another drawer and then another.

"We may not have gotten off so easily," she said. "Someone's searched my room."

The men were on their feet before Danny had finished speaking. On their feet and across the hall, the novelist drawn along in their wake.

When the lights had been switched on, they saw that Kerry's passport was standing as Danny's had been, on the dresser. Max produced his own from his pocket, in response to an inquiring look from Danny. Next to Kerry's was a white envelope, propped against the last, nearly empty, bottle of poteen.

"The vouchers for our return flights," Kerry said, passing the envelope to Max. He added to Frank, "We couldn't get tickets for our flight back because I didn't know exactly when it would be. The open returns really cost me." As he said this, he looked into each drawer of the dresser. "My wallet's gone. And all the traveler's checks."

"You have the counterfoils somewhere safe," Frank said, more as a prayer than a statement of fact.

"In my shaving kit," Kerry said. But when he went to look, he found them gone as well.

"Picked me clean," he concluded when his inventory was complete. "Now we know why Conneely wanted us out at Finnerman's house tonight. He wanted a clear field for this. Walking tour of Galway my ass. He was hiding close by this evening, waiting for us to go into action. He knew I wouldn't be taking my money or identification with me to Finnerman's in case the thing went sour. It would all be waiting for him here.

The common burglar."

"Look who's talking," Frank said. "He set up your sham burglary to cover for a real one. You should use that in one of your books, Danny."

"Who'd believe it?"

She should have been angry—Conneely had beaten her after all—but she was only very tired. "We financed the whole thing. The whole operation. Lal, Jeffrey, May. We paid them all, twice. We even tipped them."

"Why didn't he take your passports and our plane vouchers?" Max asked. "There's no market for them?"

"Just his way of saying thank you," Kerry suggested. Like his sister, he'd been unable to sustain his anger, but, in his case, it seemed to have been replaced by amusement.

"Good-bye and good riddance, you mean," Danny said.

Kerry put an arm around her. "One good thing: Finnerman will be fine now. I'd gotten off so light, I was sure my payback would be Finnerman kicking off. Now I know he'll be okay."

Chapter Thirty-Three

> *"Is he harboring a dark secret? If not, why not?"*
> —*Camelot Guide to Romance Writing*

Though illogical, Kerry's prediction proved to be perfectly accurate. Shortly after midnight, Frank learned through a discreet phone call to the local hospital that Finnerman had been rejected as too fit to stay the night.

The Fureys were up to receive this happy news because they'd reported their losses to the Liddles and, through them, to the Garda, the Irish police. This was done over Kerry's objections, or at least without his full support, and the resulting excitement greatly postponed the bedtime of every resident of the lodge.

They—a collective investigator now, with Danny lost in the crowd—determined that the burglars had approached the lodge and escaped again via the lake. One of the German arrivals had noticed a boat—or launch, as Kerry insisted the police constable describe it in his report—containing two old men who had behaved suspiciously. They'd most likely entered the men's room though an unsecured window and Danny's by picking the lock, a simple thing, as Kerry demonstrated.

His facility at this unsettled Mrs. Liddle almost as much as his prattling worried Danny. One thing only she managed to withhold from the official record of the evening: Kerry's act of housebreaking out beyond Maam Cross. In glossing over this, she told herself that she was respecting the wishes of Seamus

Finnerman, expressed as the ambulance men had strapped him to a gurney.

Danny was congratulating herself on this small victory—or perhaps rationalizing it one last time—as she finally prepared for bed. She was interrupted in the process of turning down her sheets by a knock on her door. She opened it eagerly, pausing only to pull on a sweatshirt, because she expected her visitor to be Frank O'Shea. It was Max Alnutt, literally hat in hand.

"I came to say good-bye," he said. "Cam is running me into Galway at first light. I can catch an airport shuttle there."

His always soft, always deep voice was softer than usual in the dim hallway. Danny thought of letting him in and then remembered the phone call from Lola. Max next touched on the subject of that call, tangentially.

"I'm sorry to leave you in the lurch, but I can't stay with Kerry tapped out. I can't afford to."

"I know," Danny said. "I talked to Lola this afternoon. Why did you tell Kerry you two had broken up?"

Max flashed a grin Danny remembered all too well, one that was mischievous and self-deprecating in equal parts. "Just floating the idea, I guess. Hearing from Kerry stirred up the feeling that I've been having more and more often."

He paused while a German in a silk robe padded past.

"It's the feeling that I'd really thrown away something good you and I had. I wanted to see you again to confirm that or shake it once and for all."

Not wanting to hear the verdict, Danny said, "It wasn't to ask me for a loan?"

Max chuckled. "That was mostly Lola's idea. I knew back in Ohio what you'd say to whatever I'd say." He replaced his ball cap. "Anyway, good luck getting home. Oh yeah, there are two more things I wanted to tell you, if you have another minute."

"Go ahead."

"Frank seems like a nice guy. I'm glad you've got that going for you. That is, I hope you give it or him, I mean, a chance. Kerry told me that you've been kind of closed in on yourself since the divorce. It's made me think of that god-awful movie of yours, *The Quiet Man*. Everything comes back to that this week."

"What about the movie reminds you of me?"

"The Duke's a boxer who's afraid to fight because he killed a man in the ring. I'm wondering if you're a woman who's afraid of a serious relationship because you and I killed one once. Don't be. That's all I wanted to say. Nothing that happened was your fault."

He leaned forward slightly as though to kiss her, but Danny stayed him with a question. "What was the other thing you wanted to tell me?"

"Oh, yeah. It's about Kerry. Do you remember me stealing a little drink of his poteen last night and you laughing at the face I made? It was water, short stuff. Plain water. I think that's most of what he's been drinking since we left Limerick."

"He's been hung over," Danny said. "Almost every morning."

Max shook his head. "I don't think so. I think that's his cover. I think he's even sicker than he's let on. I don't expect you'll ask him straight out about it. I know how you Fureys are. But be ready for trouble."

"That's what I meant about leaving you in the lurch. Sorry for that."

Then he kissed her without interruption.

CHAPTER THIRTY-FOUR

"Let your partners work things out for themselves."
—*Camelot Guide to Romance Writing*

For the second morning running, Danny failed to rise early enough to get the Liddle's lounge to herself, and on this occasion the penalty was worse than lost time with her neglected journal. For in that lounge she found Kerry in conversation with a stranger, soon introduced to her as Inspector Gwinn of the Garda.

Gwinn was a short man with the habit of balancing on the balls of his feet and thrusting out his square jaw when he spoke. An Irish Chester Morris, Danny classified him, drawing from her bottomless store of forgotten movie actors. She was able to observe this balancing act because Gwinn was on his feet, though Kerry and the third man present, Frank, were seated.

"Your brother's just been telling me of the shenanigans he pulled last night at the home of Seamus Finnerman," Gwinn said.

Danny shot useless and accusing looks at Kerry, who smiled back, and Frank, who merely shrugged.

"I told him," Gwinn continued, "that we'd take no action without a complaint from Mr. Finnerman."

"He didn't want us to tell anyone," Danny said, directing the comment to her brother as well.

"So Mr. O'Shea informed me. I'll confirm that, of course. If

192

it's true, I'll confine myself to warning Mr. Furey not to be so foolish again."

"What about Donal Conneely?" Danny asked.

"We can discuss that on our way to Screeb. I'd like to see the O'Shaughnessy farm, so called. If you don't mind a little drive."

To pass the time on that drive, Gwinn related a little of Conneely's history, eventually coming to the matter of aliases.

"Conneely is only one of the names we know him by. Cole's another. And Fitzgibbon, when he's playing an impoverished earl. But he's known as the Don by most of his friends in and out of the Garda."

"The Don?" Kerry asked from his place by Frank in the backseat. He'd been growing more and more somber as he listened, but now he brightened. "Is that short for Don Conneelione?"

"Movies again," Frank muttered.

"It's not a *Godfather* thing," Gwinn said with a token smile. "It's a play on Donal, of course, but it also means a don. You know, a schoolmaster. Conneely has been a teacher to a whole generation of young con artists. That's almost all he does anymore. Corrupt the youth. Around Galway and down south, his traditional territories. That and market a little moonshine. I'm surprised to hear he's back to bothering tourists. But then, everything about this business is a little surprising."

"What do you mean?" Danny asked from her seat beside him in the front of the unmarked car.

"The burglary of your lodge for one thing. That's not like the Don at all. Beneath his dignity. The great joy for a finagler like him is having the mark hand over his money, smiling all the while. And then there's the take itself. Not to make light of your loss, but it barely justified all the trouble the Don went to. And that's the third thing, the preparation. Did he improvise all this after running into you at Doolin's? That would have been fast work. Can you think of any way he could have been tipped to you earlier?"

Danny glanced up at the rearview mirror, looking for the reflection of her brother, the likeliest culprit. Instead, her reflected eye fell on Frank and lingered there briefly.

Kerry spoke up. "I think I'm to blame, Inspector. You mentioned that Conneely markets moonshine. You meant poteen?"

"Yes. I was just showing off my American slang for you."

"I bought some poteen in Limerick. Not from Conneely, but I chatted with the guy I bought it from for a minute or two. He could have reported the conversation to Conneely."

"You're saying that in the course of buying a bottle or two you passed along your whole itinerary and your fascination with *The Quiet Man*?"

"My brother has a gift for autobiography," Danny said, repeating an earlier observation of Frank's. She tried to catch the Irishman's eye in the mirror, but he was studying the passing view.

With Danny and Frank calling the turns, they eventually found the farm.

"I thought this might be the place you meant," Gwinn said as they stood between the rhododendroned house and the topless barn. "No O'Shaughnessy ever lived here. No one of any name's lived here for years." His manner added, "As any fool could see."

He went off to look around the place while the Fureys and Frank waited by the car. Kerry was considering again the skeleton of the unlucky sheep, once called Gertie, now nameless again forever.

To distract him, Frank said, "I was up half the night puzzling. The whole business of getting you to break in at Finner-

man's was a cover for the burglary at Liddle's. I'm fine with
that. But I'm still asking myself the question I asked you two
last night: Why did Conneely use Bridey Finnerman's story?
That exposed him to being found out, which Danny actually
did, though too late. Why didn't he just make up a name? And
pick a lonely house at random to be the place where the diary
was hid? It didn't matter to him where we were off to last night,
so long as we weren't at Liddle's."

Danny looked up from her own musing at this, but it was
Kerry who answered. "The Don was just building up a fiction
from a story he happened to know. Storytellers do that all the
time, use bits of other people's lives—and sorrows—in their
tales. Right, Danny?"

Frank said, "But don't you remember how Conneely was
that night in the restaurant when he told us Bridey's story?
How sad he got? It didn't seem to me he was just using someone
else's sorrow."

"He was selling," Kerry said. "Acting."

Danny felt her jaw go slack and saw Kerry react to that with
widened eyes.

"What now?"

"He wasn't telling someone else's story," Danny said. "He
was telling his own. He's Michael Robart grown old. The man
who traded Bridey for passage money to America."

"To Philadelphia," Frank said. "As he told us that same night.
He said he came back because he was afraid of losing his past."

"Of losing his memories of Bridey," Kerry said, closing the
circle. "Could it be true?"

Frank pounded a fist in a palm. "It has to be! Danny, you are
a wonder. This answers the question, why Finnerman's house?
Conneely was telling us his own heart's story and Finnerman
was a part of it."

"It was more than that," Danny said. She was seeing huge

vistas now and dizzy with it. "Remember those things that are bothering Gwinn? The burglary not being Conneely's style and the take being too small. If Conneely is Robart, we can explain those. The robbery at Liddle's was never the point of it all. We've been seeing everything backwards since we found out the traveler's checks were missing. Before that we had it right, remember? Kerry said that the whole thing was set up so that someone would burgle Finnerman's house. The robbery at Liddle's was a cover for that break-in. An excuse for it that would keep us from making the Conneely–Robart connection. The goal of Conneely's whole plan wasn't to rob us. It was to get us out to Finnerman's last night."

"But why?" Frank asked. "Why, if the diary part of the story was made up?"

"To harass Finnerman maybe," Danny said. "Robart has to hate the brother for buying him off all those years ago. He may even blame Finnerman for Bridey's death, as Finnerman does himself."

Kerry, who'd missed several turns in the guessing game, now surged ahead. "No. Conneely—Robart, I mean—didn't want to harass Finnerman. He wanted to kill him. He knew about Finnerman's heart condition. He wanted us to burst in there and scare the old guy. Scare him to death. That's what the robbery at Liddle's was covering up. If Finnerman had died and if Robart had been caught, he'd only have been charged with robbery, not murder. I was the murder weapon. And I almost did the job."

He shocked them into silence with this, his eyes and Danny's locked together, and Frank glancing back and forth between them. Gwinn rejoined them then. He noted the Fureys' staring match, but misinterpreted it.

"No use blaming each other," the policeman said. "The Don's a slick old bird. I wish we could offer you some hope that we'll recover your property. But it would be a false hope and not worth the having."

On that dour note, he proposed a return to Liddle's. Danny waited until they were on the N59 before asking the policeman, "Have you ever had any dealings with a man named Michael Robart?"

"None that I recall. Who is he, when he's at home?"

Kerry had already told the inspector the fantasy of Bridey Finnerman, canteen girl to the stars. Danny now gave him her true story, as related by her brother.

Gwinn said, "A sad business. I'm not familiar with it, but then it was well before my time on the force. What's the connection to the Don?"

Danny checked the backseat for objections and then plunged in. "We think the Don and Michael Robart may be one and the same man."

The inspector chewed on the idea, almost literally. "He'd be about the right age. But wouldn't people around here remember him as Robart?"

"Some might. But he was away in America for a time. Even after he came back, he might have avoided this area for years."

"I suppose I could check. If this Robart was enough of a hellion to have a police record, we might still have his prints."

CHAPTER THIRTY-FIVE

*"Early in Part Three, your heroine must make the decision that
will determine her ultimate fate."*
—*Camelot Guide to Romance Writing*

The inspector dropped them in Liddle's front lot. He got out of
the car himself to scribble his home number on the back of a
business card, which he passed to Danny. Kerry had moved out
of the range of another lecture by hurrying into the lodge, with
Frank trailing behind him.

Danny had her own motive for staying behind: a last question
for Gwinn. "Do you think you could find out if McFall is still in
the area?"

"The truck driver who ran the girl down? What do you want
from him?"

"His side of the story. It's all we have to show for all of this,
the story. I'm a writer."

"So your brother said. I'll see what I can do."

Danny smiled, ingratiatingly, she hoped. "I've another favor
to ask. It's for a fellow countryman of yours."

"Mr. O'Shea?" The policeman was suddenly balancing on the
balls of his feet again.

"Yes." Danny told him of Frank's troubles with the infamous
Harty Doan. "It's mostly our fault. It would be great if Frank
could go home again without walking into a beating, when this
is all over."

"You've crammed a lot into your week," Gwinn observed. "I'll make a phone call, shall I?"

"Thanks."

When Danny finally entered the lodge, she did so warily, like a person on the lookout for an ambush. In fact, a snare awaited her, not set by Frank or her brother or even Donal Conneely but by Cam Liddle himself.

The fishing expert was exiting the breakfast room, where his German guests, back from an introductory cruise on the lake, had just refortified. Liddle carried a tray of their dishes, piled high, which made his attempt to casually chat up Danny all the more transparent.

"Did you find anything at Screeb? No? Well, you wouldn't expect to, not in Screeb, a little bump in the road like that. Nor here either, for that matter. Crime and criminals, I mean. We sometimes hear of things happening to the tourists, of people taking advantage of them, but nothing like that has ever happened here. At the lodge, I mean. It was no surprise to us to learn that your troubles had followed you here. I mean, we get fishermen mostly and we're that out of the way. At least you had a fine morning for your drive. You should have been out on the lake with us. It might have still been August, for the weather. Very fine."

He'd been shifting his burden all through this without finding a balance. He shifted it once more and said, "Have you given any thought to your next stop? The thing of it is, we've a big group coming in, with the fine weather and all, maybe as early as tomorrow. . . ."

Danny, who had been fighting alternating urges—wanting to help Liddle steady his tray one moment and dash it from his nervous hands the next—felt enormous relief. She'd been waiting for this second shoe to drop ever since the police had been called. Now that shoe had struck her squarely on the head, but she felt lighter for it.

"As it happens," she said, "we were thinking of checking out today. Sorry about the short notice."

"Not at all," Liddle said. "Not at all."

He hurried off, and Danny stood on, pondering. Even without this prod, leaving Oughterard was the obvious move, but where would they go? The obvious answer was Leenane, nearest point of civilization to ethereal Letterfenny. But finding Letterfenny meant the end of their trip, and Danny found that prospect strangely unattractive.

Honest woman that she was, she forced herself to examine this sea change in her feelings. Since boarding the plane in New York, her one goal had been to board a flight back. But no longer. What had altered her so?

Danny was honest, but, like every human being, her honesty had an effective range. She got this far and no farther: She wanted to stay in Ireland because of Frank O'Shea. What she wanted beyond that—or hoped or dreamt or feared—she would consider later.

Cam Liddle bustled back just then without his tray. "The telephone for you, Ms. Furey. Inspector Gwinn."

He led her to the tiny office where she had faced down Lola only the day before. Gwinn was poised to speak as soon as he heard the line picked up.

"Ms. Furey? That truck driver you asked about, McFall, Thomas McFall, is dead. Passed away in 1996, natural causes. His widow, Grace, lives out west of here on Cashel Bay. No children apparently."

Danny pictured the inspector with square jaw thrust forward as he gave his report. "That was fast work," she said. "You must have a good computer."

"I've something better, a sergeant who's lived here all his life.

I reached him by radio. He's heard of Michael Robart, by the way, but never met him. So he couldn't help with that guess of yours that Robart grew up to be the Don. But I'll do some more checking when I get to my office. Can I reach you there for a day or two?"

"No, we're moving on."

"To Cashel Bay, by chance?"

"By chance. Know a good place?"

Danny prepared herself for some sound advice involving a trip south to the airport, but after a pause, Gwinn merely said, "You won't do better than the Bay House. Good day now."

Cam Liddle was hovering in the hallway, politely out of earshot of the conversation but clearly anxious regarding it. Concerned that the inspector had asked them to stay put, Danny decided. The American put him at his ease at once by asking for his help contacting the Bay House.

He placed the call and stood by again as Danny made the reservation, in case it was necessary to phone a second choice. The innkeeper seemed fascinated by the sight of Danny's credit card, which the American had removed from her wallet to secure the reservation. The worn piece of silver plastic fascinated Danny as well. In her case it was because the card was all that stood between herself and the now dreaded flight back, a thought to prompt philosophical musings. By way of putting an end to these, she handed the credit card to the hovering Liddle, who hurried off with it.

Five minutes later, when Danny knocked on the door to her brother's room, her mood had rebounded. Kerry answered her knock, drying one ear with a towel.

"How fast can you get packed?" Danny asked.

"I'm almost there," Kerry said. "Frank had what he called an 'inkling.' Something about a sideways look Mrs. Liddle gave him."

"You were right," Danny said, addressing the recipient of the sideways look, who had come up behind Kerry, suitcase in hand. "They want us out of here."

"What about our tab?" Kerry asked.

"Taken care of. Robart didn't get *my* wallet. I'll handle things from here out."

If Kerry understood the larger implications of this, he underreacted to them, merely raising his eyebrows.

"So it's off to Leenane at last?" Frank asked.

"Not right away. I'll tell you about it in the car."

They were on the road soon afterward, Danny having so few clean clothes left to refold. The only good-byes they received came from Kelsey, but those were heartfelt and wet. The old dog hobbled after them to the Ford, licking at their hands.

CHAPTER THIRTY-SIX

"All the pathways of your plot must lead to a Slough of Despond, *from which a happy ending seems impossible."*
—*Camelot Guide to Romance Writing*

Once again they drove west on the N59. Again and for the last time together. Danny, in the navigator's position, waited to be questioned on her new arrangements, but no questions came. Frank was once again behind the wheel, but his mind seemed elsewhere. Kerry, in the backseat, was also distracted, but contentedly so, humming to himself and smiling.

They had their choice of either going south to the coast road and then winding west or continuing west on the N59, that spine of the peninsula, and turning south at Sraith Salach. That is to say, Danny had the choice, as she'd yet to inform the others of their final destination. She chose to direct them due west, avoiding Screeb and its skeletons, real and not.

At Sraith Salach, Danny called for the left to Cashel Bay without drawing a question, but a mile down the road they were stopped by a cow—a red one—standing undecided in the road.

As they awaited the results of its deliberations, Kerry finally asked, "So are you going to tell us where we're headed? If you're planning to drive us back to New Jersey, we need to talk."

"We're stopping at a place called Cashel Bay," Danny replied. Deciding not to mention Gwinn's recommendation, she fell back on the man who had seconded it. "Cam Liddle called it 'a lovely spot.' "

"So we know the fishing's good," Frank remarked dryly.

Presently the cow moved on, and they continued to a signpost pointing right. They'd no sooner made the turn than they found themselves at the head of a rocky, irregular bay that was dotted with clumps of green island, each island resting on its perfect reflection in the still blue water.

"My apologies to Mr. Liddle," Frank said.

He had stopped the car on a high spot in the road so they could view the scene without interference from the hedgerows. Even Kerry, a man oblivious to any scenery not previously blessed by John Ford, took an interest. He pointed to their left, to a long humpbacked hill, smaller than the Connemara mountains and greener, that held the southern shore of the bay in check.

"See all those gray lines up there? Looks like graph paper. Could they be walls?"

"Could be and are," Frank said. "What's left of walls. If you're ever stuck on why your grandparents emigrated, think of that hill. Land no one in his right mind would want, divided and subdivided over and over again, until the plots wouldn't feed their owners."

He slipped the car into gear and eased them down the hill. At its bottom, they found a sign for the hotel and a drive choked with fuchsia. These shrubs brushed their windows on either side, obscuring their view of everything except the sharply climbing track. As they neared the top, the drive turned, and they saw Bay House as its builder had intended it to be seen: commanding its little rise.

It was a mansion and not a house, its walls a brilliant white, its roof slate. The design was asymmetrical: a two-story center structure, its unadorned gable facing them, and to its left a series of three wings, each one set back a little from the previous one so that it was possible to speculate, as Danny speculated, that the first wing was part of the original design of the house and the two setbacks later additions. If so, they were perfectly matched additions, each with the same windows—rounded on the upper story, plain on the bottom story, and all trimmed in robin egg's blue—the same slate roofs, the same white chimneys. Each section had its own trellis of roses, the red blooms almost reaching as high as the blue guttering. Balancing all of this to the right of the anchoring center structure was a little glassed-in portico with a continuously curving wall and a roof as flat as Liddle's.

Behind the building was a line of wispy pines, half again as tall as the house, and behind them one of the gray-green mountains they'd skirted on their drive.

"Next trip you make all the arrangements, Sis," Kerry said as they unpacked the car.

Danny didn't reply, being preoccupied with the arrival of bellhops, the first real ones they'd encountered in Ireland.

The Americans and Frank walked empty-handed into the hotel, past a turf fire just inside the hall, past the entrance to a spacious dining room that extended into the glassed portico, and on to the front desk, which was nestled beneath a staircase and staffed by a woman scarcely older than Rose, Kerry's beloved rental car agent. Her brass name tag identified her only as Deidre. When she welcomed them to the Bay House, Danny heard an accent, of course, but one that was not Irish, but French.

Kerry's interest in this and in Deidre herself, who was all of six feet tall with skin the color of caramel, extended the check-in process. A further delay was caused by Frank, who insisted on booking and paying for his own room.

"I've had enough of dormitory life," he explained to Danny.

Kerry was still bantering with Deidre as she led them up the stairs, the loaded bellhops bringing up the rear. Once above, they followed Deidre down a hallway that jogged as the building jogged. Just past the second of these offsets, she stopped at the first of their three rooms.

The space she showed them into was almost a suite, with a bath to the left of the entry, a spacious bedroom beyond, and a sitting room beyond that, set off from the rest by a curtained archway. These curtains featured a bold floral pattern, as did the wallpaper and the spread of the king-size bed. The upholstered pieces were red velvet and the carpet grass green.

"All three rooms are the same," she said, "except that the first two connect and the third, on the end of the house, has an extra window."

"That window one's for me," Kerry said. "I've been feeling vitamin D deficient since we got off the plane."

He walked off with his appointed bellhop before anyone else could say a word.

"I'll act as buffer state, then," Frank said, taking the room in the middle.

When her bags had been deposited and their bearers tipped, Danny asked a question of Deidre. "How would I go about finding a woman who lives in Cashel Bay named Grace Mc-Fall?"

"We've some local girls on the staff," Deidre replied, showing no more curiosity than she had on the question of the connecting rooms. "Let me ask them."

She made a turn like a pirouette and was gone. Before Danny could close her door, she heard an impertinence from Kerry and Deidre's patient laugh. Then her brother was barging past her.

"I'm missing a bag, Sis. The little plaid one that has my

mobile pharmacy in it. There it is, right there. Sorry to bother you."

"How about your poteen?" Danny asked.

Kerry gave her only the merest sideways glance. "It survived the trip, what's left of it. Care for a snort?"

While she was trying to decide whether to call this bluff, a soft knock sounded on the connecting doors. Kerry unbolted and opened Danny's door without being asked. Beyond it, Frank's door already stood open, with the man himself in its place.

"I thought I heard a conference in here," he said. "What's the plan? And whatever it is, I hope it includes an early dinner. Our meals have become as irregular as homespun lately."

Both men turned to Danny, who replied, "I'm hoping to interview the widow of Thomas McFall, the man who ran down Bridey Finnerman."

"You are?" Kerry replied with gratifying surprise. "Why exactly?"

Again, Danny balked at mentioning the haunting she'd been party to. She said instead, "I'm still trying to figure out what Conneely was really up to."

Kerry cocked his head but said only, "Good idea. You two can go visiting after we eat. I'll stay here. I think Deidre wants to get to know me better."

The men left her, Frank shutting his connecting door as he went. Danny waited to hear the sound of his deadbolt being thrown, but heard nothing. She contemplated her own door's lock for a time, even reaching for it once. Reaching for, but not actually touching.

CHAPTER THIRTY-SEVEN

"Give your readers what they want, but not what they expect."
—*Camelot Guide to Romance Writing*

After their early dinner, Danny and Frank set out, down the fuchsia-chocked drive with barely room for a bicycle to pass them safely and out onto the barely wider road that followed the edge of the bay, the surface of which could be glimpsed through gaps in a wild hedge. The tide was out, and the rocky bank was covered in seaweed the color of new copper. Beyond that the water—still but for a tickle of wind playing here and there—was picking up the pink of the western sky and deepening almost to a rose. The pink deepened in the sky itself as they drove—Danny more conscious of the crimson clouds almost than the road—so that, when they found themselves at length at the crossroads she had been told to expect, it seemed to her they'd barely moved from the hotel.

Yet there was the cottage they sought, the McFall cottage, described to Danny by its owner during a phone call placed with Deidre's help, during which Mrs. McFall had agreed to an evening appointment, much to Danny's relief. The little house looked so familiar to her that she felt she'd surely been there before. Frank had parked the Ford and they'd climbed out before the answer came to her. The square block building was very like May O'Shaughnessy's house, or rather the house she'd claimed as hers. Except that this place had been painted recently and the shrubbery was well under control.

Danny saw a figure framed in an open doorway at the head of steep front steps. Mrs. McFall, ready to slam the door on them if she didn't like their looks, Danny decided. She smiled up at the woman hopefully.

Mrs. McFall turned out to be as trim as her estate and as tiny, her height no more than five one. Her current height, one might say, for she must have been taller once; her back was badly bowed with age. Her brown hair was cut short and worn as carelessly as a child's, but the hollow-cheeked face beneath it was that of an old and sorely used soul.

The widow showed them into her house after asking no more than their names. As Danny sat, she worded a polite rejection of the inevitable offer of tea, but no such offer came.

"You're an American author then," Mrs. McFall said to her. "And you're interested in the story of Bridey Finnerman."

"Yes," Danny said. She'd adhered strictly to the truth during their brief phone conversation.

"The *true* story of her death?"

"Yes."

Much of the room's light came from a large old television set. Mrs. McFall had turned down the sound when she'd shown her visitors into the room but had left the picture going. Danny and Frank sat on either side of the set, where neither could see the program. The widow's own chair was set squarely before the glowing tube, and she was lit irregularly by its flickering as though by the palest of fires.

"What do you write, young woman?"

"Romantic stories."

"Ah. I understand your interest in Bridey Finnerman. Who sent you to me?"

Again the strict truth. "Father Rich, over at St. Timothy's, mentioned your husband's name."

"Father Rich? You can't have got a very complete history from him. How did he say the girl died?"

"He said she was run over by a truck."

Mrs. McFall's sharp reply took Danny by surprise.

"All the world knows that, girl. How did the priest say she came to be under the wheels of the truck?"

She'd said the word *priest* with a little hiss in the middle, Danny noted. "He said there was some question about that."

"Did he?" She sat back for a moment. "Very liberal of him. Must be the influence of Vatican II being felt in the west of Ireland at last. Certainly there was no doubt as to why she'd died when it happened. Not among Father Rich's crony priests. It was all the fault of my husband Thomas, the drunkard."

"Had he been drinking that night?" Frank asked.

"He'd had a pint with his dinner. But what was that in 1958? Who among the police who came to investigate him or the people who accused him hadn't had their own pint and more that very night? If you're asking me was he drunk, he was not. If you're asking was the accident his fault, it was not."

The novelist was perplexed by the old woman's vehemence. "How did your husband say the accident came to happen?"

Just then, the television lit the room brightly for an instant. Danny saw the widow react to what she clearly took to be a foolish question. "It was night. It was foggy. The road was no bigger than the one you came here on and winding. The girl was in the road."

"Your husband saw her standing there too late to stop?" Frank asked.

"He never saw her, not alive. And I never said she was standing. She was *in* the road, lying in the road, waiting to be killed, wanting to be killed, the selfish creature. Never thinking what her selfish act would do to the man behind the wheel of that truck, how it would blight his life. How he'd lose his reputation and his job and almost lose his mind with the nightmares of her bloody corpse.

"None of that would have happened to him if they'd just called the thing what it was. But no. It had to be an accident caused by drink, so she could be buried where she had no business being buried. In consecrated earth. My Thomas's life ruined so that no man could say what every man knew: The selfish girl had taken her own life."

"Because she was pregnant?" Danny asked.

"Don't tell me a priest told you that."

"Was she pregnant?"

"Who could know that now?"

"Then what proof do you have that Bridey was a suicide?"

"Proof? She's given us proof of that herself. Not a year goes by without her adding to it. She's the famous ghost of her parish. Been seen over and over again walking the roads on foggy nights. Father Rich didn't mention that, did he? Not him, not for all his liberality. Too upsetting to his theology. But I'd bet my soul he's seen her."

Danny, remembering Father Rich's own qualms regarding the peace of Bridey's rest, declined to take the wager.

Mrs. McFall seemed to read her thoughts and picked up where the priest's musings had left off. "Why else would she be walking the earth after all these years? She who's safe in the shadow of a church? It can only be that she has no right to be there. That she was put there wrongfully and has gotten no good from it."

CHAPTER THIRTY-EIGHT

"It always comes down to sex—or you're not doing it right."
—*Camelot Guide to Romance Writing*

They sat staring for a time while the silent television cast its campfire light about the room.

Then Danny asked, "Have you seen her? Bridey?"

"I have not," Mrs. McFall said, with what sounded to the novelist like sincere regret. It took no effort at all for her to picture the widow haranguing a ghost. Or the devil himself.

"Do any of the people who see her say how she's dressed?" Double-checking still, with a dry mouth.

If their hostess thought the question odd, she didn't show it, giving it her standard contempt and nothing more. "All of them say how she's dressed, since it's the only way to identify her, she comes and goes so quickly. She wears what she died in: an old plain coat and a bit of blue silk over her hair."

Frank asked, "Did your husband ever see Bridey's ghost?"

"No. That was the only kindness she ever showed him, she who ruined his life. Not that he'd ever say a word against her. Not Thomas. None of his suffering was her fault. It was all the fault of the fog and the other."

"The other?" Danny prompted.

"The one who never came forward. The one Thomas saw while he was standing over the girl in the road. The fog parted like a rent sheet and there he was, standing on a hillock staring down at them. Thomas called to the man for help, but he just stood there, as stiff and distant as God the Father. Then the fog mended itself, and he was gone.

"Thomas expected the man to come forward and tell what he'd seen, but he never did. And the police never found him, if they even looked, what with Thomas in hand and the priests all working to bury the truth along with the girl."

"What did the other look like?"

"Thomas could never say. He'd only seen him for a second and he'd been near to shock. But he always expected the man to identify himself. He expected it through years of working on a road crew cutting weeds, the only job he could find. He died expecting it."

No such illusion comforted his widow, Danny realized. They thanked the old woman and stood to go. She got up quickly to see them out, turning on light after light now that her company was leaving. The last she switched on was a light on a wooden post that lit her front steps. The fixture wore a fat halo of mist.

"A fog's coming," she said, sniffing the air. "They come up fast with the bay so near. It's the kind of night Bridey fancies. Maybe you'll have her company on your drive home."

It'd be a welcome change, Danny thought. She said, "Thanks for your time."

It wasn't a fog yet, only the makings of one. Still, Frank drove carefully, perhaps with Thomas McFall's example in the back of his mind.

He slowed even more when Danny said, "Now we have the whole story."

"We do?"

She thought for a moment of waiting to tell this complete tale until Kerry was with them, but only for a moment. "Conneely was 'the other.' Michael Robart was, I mean. He killed

Bridey and put her body in the road. Or he put her there while she was still breathing and let the truck finish her off."

"Why would he do that?"

"She'd ruined the bargain he'd struck with Seamus Finnerman. Finnerman had promised to pay Robart's way to a new life in America, but he hadn't paid him yet. Remember, he said that Robart's money came from Bridey's insurance."

"And how had she threatened that?"

"By getting pregnant. Finnerman wouldn't have paid the baby's father to desert Bridey, no matter how big a lowlife he was. He'd have had the banns announced the Sunday next."

"Wait now, wait. You're getting way ahead of me and ahead of yourself as well. How do you know Bridey was pregnant? As Grace McFall just said, no one could know that now. The whole idea of a pregnancy was just something Conneely threw in way back when Bridey was supposedly working on a movie crew."

"Exactly," Danny said. "It was a detail of the real story Conneely worked into his phony one. That's how we know she was pregnant. The only man on earth who knows it for sure told us."

"But why?" Frank asked, returning to his complaint of the evening before. "Why use Bridey's story? It was too big a risk when we thought this was all about a con. But if it was murder, the risk is a hundred times more. Using Bridey would practically be a confession."

The remark so delighted Danny that she reached for Frank's hand on the gearshift and squeezed it. "That's it. This whole thing was a confession. It wasn't a con, it wasn't a way to hit back at Finnerman, it was a confession. Conneely might not even have seen that himself."

"Evidently not," Frank said, "since he walked away with your brother's money."

Danny barely heard him. She'd been scanning the night for

Bridey from what was now old habit. When she looked to the road again, she saw the sign for the hotel and the mist-blurred form of a young woman beside it. Frank must have seen her, too, since he braked sharply, even as Danny was cataloging the reasons why this couldn't be the dead girl. This one wore a hooded windbreaker above a short dark skirt. And held a cigarette. A second later, the specter was joined by two more, similarly dressed. Workers from the hotel, Danny realized, heading home at the end of their shift.

The three women were considering their headlights suspiciously. Danny reached over and switched on the turn signal to indicate that their destination was Bay House. Immediately the three took up their talking and laughing again and headed off down the road.

CHAPTER THIRTY-NINE

*"Impossible challenge number two: Make the worst possible
thing that can happen to your heroine the best possible thing."*
—*Camelot Guide to Romance Writing*

Deidre was still at her post behind the cubbyhole desk and
sleepy-eyed, until she saw Danny. She roused herself to push a
message slip across the counter. It was from Gwinn, asking
Danny to call him at home.

"I'll go check on his nibs," Frank said.

Danny handed the desk clerk Gwinn's business card and
asked her to place the call. Deidre showed her to a discreet
phone in a little cubicle off the bar, saying, "I'll ring you here
when I've reached him."

Danny listened to a foursome of Americans in the bar proper
discussing the day's horseback riding. Then the barman stuck
his head around her corner to ask if she wanted anything.

"Bushmills," the novelist said.

The man returned carrying a salver on which were balanced
two glasses, one containing a double whiskey and another ice.
Danny accepted the neat liquor just as the phone began to ring.

She answered with "Yes," expecting it to be Deidre reporting
success or failure, but the voice that replied belonged to the
man she'd asked the clerk to reach: Inspector Gwinn of the
Garda.

"Yes what?" Gwinn said. "So you got in at the Bay House,

216

did you? Quite a step up from a fishing lodge. My wife—"

Danny broke in then. "She was murdered, Inspector."

"Who was?"

"Bridey Finnerman. The girl Conneely used in his story. The one who was run over by a truck."

She spilled it all out to him then, seeing as she did so young Michael Robart of the flinty eyes standing on a moonlit rise, waiting for a truck or car to pass.

When she'd finished, Gwinn digested for the time it took Danny to raise her glass to her lips and realize that she'd somehow emptied it while she'd talked.

Then the inspector said, "Might I remind you that we haven't even proven yet that Conneely is Robart? God knows how we'll prove any of the rest of this."

"You won't have to," Danny answered, very sure of her ground now. "Ask Conneely and he'll tell you. That's what this was all about. It wasn't to get our money. It wasn't to harass Finnerman." *Or even to kill him,* she added to herself. "It was to reopen Bridey's death so Robart would be found out at last. He wants to be found out. He wants one last chance to confess. That hit-and-run story he made up for us was nine-tenths confession.

"Just ask him, and he'll tell you everything. And thank you at the end."

"That would be a first," Gwinn said. "Now may I have the floor?"

Danny remembered belatedly that she was returning the inspector's call. "Sorry. What did you want to tell me?"

"Two things," Gwinn said, as Max had the night before. "First, I heard from Cam Liddle. He told me someone called the lodge asking after you this afternoon. Mrs. Liddle told the caller where you'd gone before her husband could stop her. She said it sounded like an old man. Conneely may be on your track."

Danny raised her empty glass again and, irritated, set it on the floor. "Maybe he wants to do his confessing to us," she said.

"I wouldn't bet too much on that. Your neck, for instance."

"Was there something else?"

"Yes. I heard from Limerick. Frank O'Shea is free to return whenever he wants."

"That's wonderful, Inspector," Danny said, though at best she felt ambivalent about it.

So did Gwinn. "Not so wonderful. Someone's been pulling your leg, and it just may be O'Shea. Harty Doan is a mate of his. Doan doesn't own a pub, he works in one. He's never been a bookmaker or broken a leg. He claims the business at the aunt's farm was a pantomime O'Shea came up with himself. Doan doesn't know what it was all about and he also denies knowing Donal Conneely. We're checking into that. It could be Conneely didn't hear of you through a moonshiner after all."

The line crackled for a time. Then Gwinn said, "Do you want me to send someone out to talk with O'Shea? Or I could drive out myself."

"No, thanks," Danny said. "I'll handle it."

She had little time to decide how. She hung up with Gwinn and started for her room, and there was Frank, waiting for her at the bottom of the stairs. She'd put the thing off until the morning, she decided, but her face betrayed her.

"You know then," he said, hanging his head like a truant schoolboy. "I've been trying to tell you since that day on the lakeshore. I should never have kissed you without telling you first. But there've been so many ex-husbands and con men underfoot—"

"And who's to blame for the con men?" Danny demanded.

His head shot back as though she'd slapped him. "Me, you

218

think? I'm in Conneely's gang?"

"What was that Harty Doan business if it wasn't a con? Your boss called Liddle's this afternoon to trace us. He may be here now."

"I admit I put Harty up to chasing us. But because of Max, not Conneely. I was that afraid he'd make you leave me behind, and I didn't want to be left behind."

He reached for her then, a fatal mistake. She brushed past him and on up the stairs.

He called after her, "If I'm Conneely's spy, why would he have to call to find you?"

CHAPTER FORTY

"Danger is the ultimate aphrodisiac."
—Camelot Guide to Romance Writing

Danny gained the upper hallway and then her door without a further word from Frank. She had locked that door behind her before she noticed someone sitting in the shadows at the far end of her room. It was an old man, armed with a black revolver. Not Donal Conneely, as she might have thought had she had time to think, but Seamus Finnerman.

"Come away from the door now," Finnerman said. He was breathing with some effort, as he'd done the night Kerry had all but killed him, and his color was almost as bad as then. He was shiny with sweat, though it was cool and the room's single widow was open. But the hand holding the gun was steady.

"Where's the other?" Finnerman demanded. "The lock picker?"

Danny forced herself not to glance at the bedside telephone that would be used to summon Kerry if she misspoke. "Down in the village. Doing the pubs."

"Then we've a wait," Finnerman said. He pointed with his great beak of a nose toward the room's other chair.

The American sat down, her knees a yard from Finnerman's. A yard and more from the gun.

Too far. "How about pointing that thing somewhere else?"

Finnerman said nothing for some minutes, until Danny

thought she'd scream. Then he roused himself.

"So you went to the Garda, did you? After I asked you not to."

"We went about Conneely," Danny replied. "Not you."

"About Michael Robart," Finnerman corrected. "Call him by his right name. Your Inspector Gwinn came by to see me. To ask about my old dealings with Robart. He told me what Black Michael's been up to. Prying into Bridey's death after all these years, using you Yanks as his cat's-paws."

The old man grinned a grin that was ridiculously dainty on his sweating slab of a face. It disappeared entirely when a knock sounded on the unlocked connecting door. Before Danny could call out a warning, the door opened and Frank strode in, carrying a bottle and two glasses. His long legs carried him well into the dark room before he saw Finnerman. Then he froze.

"Join us, driver," the old man said. "Though you look to be more than that. I hadn't thought to include you, but it may be just as well that I do."

Frank came over to stand beside Danny's chair. The bottle he carried was champagne, she saw, its foil and protective wire gone, Frank's thumb atop the cork.

"Gwinn had an idea that Robart might not be done with you," Finnerman said to Danny, breathing hard between words. "I can't have you putting your heads together. Not after you talked with that truck driver's widow. Oh yes, I know why you came here. I knew as soon as I called Liddle's and they told me you'd moved on to the Bay House."

"Gwinn knows about that call," Danny said. "You covered your tracks better in 1958."

"I had more to lose back then. The prime years of life, which is what you've been gambling away, whether or not you knew it."

Danny knew she was playing for far less time now. If only

she'd taken Gwinn up on his offer to drive out. That regret reminded her of something the inspector had said.

"I'm no threat to you. We can't prove anything now. Not after all these years. You know that better than anyone. Why did you really come here tonight?"

"Why did you go into my parlor, eh? Why did you pick up that photo of Bridey? Don't tell me you didn't. Somebody moved it. And you're the brains of the outfit. Gwinn told me that."

There seemed no reason left to feign ignorance, so she asked, "Why did you kill Bridey? You were the man Thomas McFall saw on the hill that night, not Robart. Was it because she was pregnant or because she was insured?"

Frank criticized her tactlessness with a sharp intake of breath, Finnerman with a wave of his gun.

"I'll ask the questions, girl. Why did you keep worrying at it after Robart had cut and run? You had no one prodding you after that."

"You know why. Robart wasn't the only one who's been prodding me. Or even the first."

"Who then?"

"Your sister, Bridey. The famous ghost of the parish." Danny felt sick to her stomach and increasingly detached, thinking of herself writing this same scene and wondering if she would have thought to include the nausea. "She's been dropping in on me all week. My stalker, I thought. I didn't know who she was— didn't know for sure—until that night at your house."

Finnerman's gun hand began to tremble, but whether that was a good sign or a very bad one, Danny couldn't tell.

"You're lying," the old man said. "People around here have told that lie forever just to spite me. And now you. Robart put you up to it."

"You know it's no lie. That's why you're here. She found me

in Limerick the day I got off the plane. She was so close to me at Liddle's, I could see she'd been crying."

"Bridey!" Finnerman rasped, his eyes darting around the darkening room.

"She wears an old brown coat and a bit of blue scarf over her hair. The scarf may have been bloody when you saw it last."

Finnerman was still searching the shadows. Danny was tempted to look herself, but found she couldn't take her eyes from the gun.

"Is she here now?" the old man asked, pleadingly. He struggled to his feet. "What does she want? To see me hung? Why now? Why now, Bridey?"

Danny had stood as well. She found she had an answer ready, the one she'd been saving for Conneely. "She doesn't want to see you punished. She wants you to confess. She knows you don't have much time left. She doesn't want you to die with murder on your soul."

"My soul? She was my soul. Bridey, Bridey, where are you? Bridey, I'm sorry. I was desperate for money. Barely hanging on. I'd sacrificed so much for you. For your schooling. You could have made a fine match. You could have been the saving of me. But you threw it all away on a worthless man. Bridey!"

He was looking past Danny's shoulder and deep into one corner of the room. Focusing now on something there. Danny was steeling herself to swing at the gun when the bottle in Frank's hand went off like a toy cannon. The cork struck Finnerman in the face and then Frank was on him.

The connecting door burst open behind them. Into the room came Kerry, two Garda constables, and one other. Donal Conneely.

CHAPTER FORTY-ONE

"A love scene is like a fish: best served
without the head and tail."
—Camelot Guide to Romance Writing

Much later, Danny and Frank had the same room to themselves. A very pale but strangely triumphant Kerry had been packed off to bed. Seamus Finnerman had been taken away by the constables and Donal Conneely as well, though it was Conneely himself who had arranged for the police to be there, or so he claimed. He'd used himself as bait, calling the local constabulary to report that the notorious Don could be taken at the Bay House, and then persuading the officers, with Kerry and Frank's desperate help, that there was a bigger prize to be caught there. The Garda men had happily netted Finnerman but had declined to toss Conneely back.

"The Don followed Finnerman out here this evening," Frank explained for the third time, standing near the still open connecting doors with Danny close beside him. "I guess he's had Finnerman's house watched since the night Kerry broke in, hoping the old man would do something to give himself away."

"Like shooting us," Danny said. "You knew Finnerman was in there and you still came in—"

Frank affected a shrug and almost pulled it off. "You're the brains of the outfit. We'd be lost without you."

"—armed with a well-shaken champagne bottle."

"I had it in my room anyway. I'd ordered it earlier."

"Before I'd decided you were Conneely's stooge."

"Henchman," Frank said.

"How early did you order the champagne?"

"Before dinner. I thought we might—"

"Tell me again why you dreamt up the business with Harty Doan."

"To stay near you," he said, drawing nearer still.

"When did you know?"

He came very close indeed then and kissed her, answering her rash and impertinent question—since when?—with the same act and dismissing even rasher and more impertinent ones, such as why me? Those kisses filled the longing that she'd scarcely been willing to admit to herself, one she now realized had been with her since her first glimpse of Frank at Durty Nelly's. And so for him as well, she understood him to say, though neither of them spoke. So for him since that first night.

When they'd finished, he took a reluctant step backward toward his room. "You want me to bolt the door?"

"Yes," Danny said. "From this side."

They made love then in the same privacy Danny had always afforded her fictional characters: the space between two pages.

Chapter Forty-Two

"Don't know your story's destination?
You could be heading for trouble."
      —*Camelot Guide to Romance Writing*

Their departure from the Bay House the next morning was
delayed by a last interview with Inspector Gwinn. Toward the
end of their talk, the Garda man expressed his opinion that
Finnerman would never be formally punished for his sister's
murder, given the lack of real evidence, the old man's age, and
his condition, physical and mental. However, the penalty for
holding Frank and Danny at gunpoint would itself amount to a
life sentence, in Gwinn's opinion, however lenient the judge.

A mute witness to this interview was Donal Conneely,
brought back to the scene by the inspector. Though Kerry had
dropped charges with a will, Gwinn had insisted on keeping
Conneely at hand until all could be sorted out. The Don sat
through Gwinn's talk with the Americans and Frank in
uncharacteristic silence. And with a sad smile on his haggard
face.

They said good-bye to the policeman and the tour guide
outside the hotel. The morning was so still that Danny could
hear the faint creak of oarlocks from a boat far off on the bay.
Conneely came to her last, as the novelist had been hanging
back, and the old man led her away from the group a further
step or two.

"So you've really seen her? Bridey?"

"Yes."

"I never have, though I've heard the stories of it and looked and looked. I can't say I blame her for avoiding me after the way I betrayed her. I did, you know. That part of Finnerman's story is perfectly true."

Danny was near to dispensing forgiveness in Bridey's name again. Sensing that, perhaps, Conneely hurried on.

"I'm sorry for putting you three in danger for the sake of my answers. But Finnerman and I are so old now. I was afraid if I waited any longer to press the thing, I'd miss my last chance. And you and your brother were a heaven-sent chance."

"You suspected Finnerman all along?"

"No. At first I was too drunk with my own guilt to suspect anyone of anything. But later, much later. . . . Still, I had no right to put you at hazard. I had a bit of trouble with a tire yesterday, or I would have been here to spring the trap before Finnerman had gotten you alone. Thank God it all worked out."

Gwinn was very obviously anxious to be off, but Conneely stood on, gazing out at the water. "Will you tell this story, young Danny?"

"I don't know. I might."

"You should. It may be important for you to. It may even be the point of it all. Though you'll probably disguise it beyond recognizing. I know how you book writers are. And you'll make poor Bridey some figment of your imagination or something you ate on the flight over that troubled your digestion.

"When *I* tell it, and tell it I will—you'll hear my voice in your head, in fact, when you get around to telling it yourself—Bridey will be a ghost, nothing more and nothing less. No Irish audience will expect an apology for that. And I'll tell it just as it happened and make all of us who we are, though I may end up a wee bit taller. And a dead ringer for some actor or other."

"Douglas Fairbanks, Jr.," Danny said.

"I thank you."

He sniffed the air, as Grace McFall had done. "You'll have a perfect day for your expedition. And that brings me to what I really wanted to say. You must promise to write me care of Egan's Pub in Ennis to tell me what you find up in your Letterfenny."

"I don't expect to find anything," Danny said.

"What did you expect to find when you came to Ireland last week? And look what you're going away with. That's what your expecting is worth. I need a proper ending for my story, girl. And you're the only one who can give it to me. Promise!"

They shook on it, spitting on their hands first like two Irish movie characters. Then Conneely was gone.

CHAPTER FORTY-THREE

"Make Newton proud: For every action,
have an equal and opposite reaction."
—*Camelot Guide to Romance Writing*

Danny was still watching the empty drive when Kerry approached her.

"I think I'm ready to go home, Sis. It's been a great week, but I'm pretty bushed. This will work out great. You can drop me at the Shannon Airport on your way to meet Frank's family. I should be along for that, but like I said, I'm bushed."

Danny looked him in the eye. "Are you sure you're just tired?"

Kerry met her gaze without the least evasion. "Absolutely."

"Good. Then we're going to Letterfenny. You can sleep on the way. I promised Donal we'd see this through."

After a moment's further staring, Kerry shrugged. "Your call."

By late morning they were rolling north through a pass in the Maamturk Mountains—black and threatening in a sudden rain. By and by they met their old friend the N59, which had traveled west as far as Clifden without them, arched north and then east, and had met them here on the far side of the Maamturks. Frank made a right turn onto it, away from the signs for Kylemore Abbey and toward the ones for Leenane.

A few curves later Killary Harbor came into view, that true arm of the sea, though narrow as a river and miles long. Beyond the silver water, the mountains of County Mayo appeared, distant at first but marching closer and closer as the harbor narrowed. By the time they sighted Leenane, the green giants had reached the water's very edge, forming an Irish fjord with the town at its head.

They parked the Ford at the seawall that edged the harbor, and together they gazed down Killary's length. The rain they'd driven through was on the horizon now, creating the illusion that the harbor was emptying itself into a black tunnel.

Kerry said to Frank, "I know you're right about the living being hard here way back when. Still. When I stand here I have to wonder how our ancestors could have torn themselves away."

Danny said, "It must have killed them to think back on this."

"Too right," Frank said.

Opposite the seawall stood a building of recent construction but old materials—field stone and slate—so that it might have slipped unnoticed into its surroundings but for the parking lot to its left, which had been designed to hold tour buses. Two were idling in their diagonal spaces at that moment, Danny belatedly noticed.

" 'Leenane Cultural Center,' " she read from the sign above the building's arched entryway. "That wasn't here ten years ago."

Kerry chuckled. "We must have forgotten to tell them to keep everything exactly the way we'd last seen it. Shall we inquire within?"

The interior of the center was a combination of gift shop, snack bar, and museum, and as crowded with tourists as the street outside had been empty. Luckily just then a demonstration of sheep herding was announced. Most of the crowd filed out an exit that led to an outdoor exhibition area.

The Fureys and Frank looked on briefly through a window as a small black-and-white dog ran a dozen sheep around a meadow, Kerry observing, "That's just the way the Don handled us."

And you me, Danny thought. "Now's our chance," she said aloud.

She led them to a counter where a beleaguered clerk was enjoying a brief respite. The man's distinguishing features were two bushy sideburns of the type popular three decades earlier and a full century before that.

Disregarding the sigh with which they were greeted, Danny said, "We're trying to find a village near here called Letterfenny. A former village, I mean. It's been deserted since World War I. We haven't been able to locate it on any of our maps."

"Letterfenny," the clerk repeated with no recognition in his very soft voice. "Would those be road maps you've been checking?"

Danny nodded.

"You might want to try an ordinance map. They show all the old mountain villages, the old tracks and trails. The hikers swear by them." He nodded to a display case. "We're not supposed to use them ourselves. . . ."

"We'll take one," Frank said.

"Right. We'll need number thirty-seven, Galway and Mayo." He retrieved the map and spread it out on his counter.

"Now we're getting somewhere," Kerry said, running his hand along the map's border. "Latitudes and longitudes."

"You know the latitude and longitude of Letterfenny then?" the clerk asked.

"Ignore him," Danny advised. "All we know is the people of the village used to walk down for mass to a chapel on the Kylemore road."

"I know the old chapel," the clerk said. "It's just a ruin now, trees growing through its roof. Somewhere about here." He ran his finger down the N59, which was white with green stripes, a single instance of whimsy on the otherwise humorless map. "That would put Letterfenny—"

"There," Danny said, spotting the word in tiny type and feeling an unexpected thrill. "Right above your finger."

"You're kidding," Kerry said, crowding in.

"So it is," said the clerk. "Well done. But how to get you there? The map shows no road or trail. You could park by the old chapel and walk up, but you might easily lose your way."

A second clerk had joined them, an older man more conventionally side-whiskered. "That's the Reagan property," he said. "All that there between those little lakes, Lough Nacarrigeen and Nambrackkeagh. You don't want to send them walking back in there unless they've spoken with Ned Reagan first. Sheep," he added to Danny. "Sheep and more sheep. That track they show there to the east of your village—see that line of dashes?—that's the drive to his house."

"There you are," the first clerk said. "Ned Reagan's the man you want to see. Drive west on the N59 until you see his sign. You'll never miss it. That will be seven and ten for the map. Thank you. Can I interest you in anything else?"

"Something to keep out the cold," Danny said.

"A wee dram?" the clerk asked, puzzled.

"Yes," Kerry said.

"No," Danny said, pointing to her brother. "A rain jacket. Size him."

Chapter Forty-Four

"Great obstacles make great heroines."
—Camelot Guide to Romance Writing

They found Ned Reagan in his barn—a fine big stone barn with an intact roof. The drive to the property had been uneventful and even direct, by the standards of their wandering week. A few miles outside the village, they'd spotted the sign for the farm, or rather for "Reagan's Purebred Sheep." They'd turned onto a lane very like Liddle's, except that Liddle's had gently descended to lake level while this one had gently climbed.

Presently they'd come to a compound of barn and outbuildings and house, with a central courtyard of packed clay still crossed by rivulets of the latest shower. A dog had greeted them, a near relation of the one who performed for the tourists in Leenane. The little animal had guided them—herded them, Danny couldn't help thinking—to the open barn and Reagan.

The dog's master was seated on a box, surrounded by pieces of a disassembled something. A washing machine, Danny realized, when her mind had had time to work the puzzle. Reagan held his hand out to Frank. In greeting, Danny thought. But when he had the redhead firmly clasped, Reagan used him as a counterweight and pulled himself to his feet.

He was a tall man topped with a twin of Conneely's flat cap and dressed in greasy overalls with bits of greasy sweater visible at the throat and the sleeve ends. A hatchet-faced man, and the hatchet all dirty but for its very tip, the hooked nose, which shone. From that Danny deduced that the man had a cold and had been wiping his nose all morning while ignoring the rest of him. Sure enough, he wiped it as soon as he was steady on his feet, using a handkerchief he pulled from an unseen back pocket.

"Much obliged," the sheep man said to Frank. "Two Americans and a what?" he asked Frank. This though they'd each said no more than hello.

"The Americans' keeper," Frank said.

Reagan smiled at that, revealing merry eyes that greatly reduced the sharpness of his aspect. "Know anything about washing machines?"

"Only that we could really use one," Kerry said.

"Sorry," Danny said. "We don't."

"No matter. Come to see the holy well, have you? Or was it the megalithic tomb?"

"The well," Kerry said.

"Letterfenny," Danny said and firmly.

"Letterfenny?" Reagan repeated amazed. "However did you Yanks—and your keeper—hear of that little place?"

Danny traced for him the branch of their lineage that led backward to the village, being careful not to sound like a rightful heir returned to claim her lands.

"Ah, well, you're welcome to go there of course. But it's a long walk and not much to see at the end. A nice grove of trees your ancestors planted and a few shattered buildings is all. Truth to tell, the holy well and the old tomb—that the hikers are always asking to see, you know—aren't much either. But at least they're closer by."

"This well," Kerry said. "Is it associated with any miraculous cures?"

Danny felt herself outmaneuvered, and at the very end of the game. But Reagan whistled the play dead.

"None at all," he said. "And I've tested the thing scientifically, on myself and on the sheep." Here he wiped his nose again. "It's not even what you'd call unique. We've so much holy water in this part of the country, the Vatican is jealous. Though I've never understood how any source of water came to be venerated in a place where you can't stay dry two days running. I could understand it in the Sahara."

"So could I," Danny said. "I guess we'll stick with Letterfenny."

"You've boots," Reagan said to Frank with an admiring look at his footwear. "But what about your charges? No? Well, I'll set you up. I've some old Wellingtons you're welcome to borrow. They'll keep out the damp."

"How close can we get by car?" Kerry asked as Reagan rooted in a dark corner for the boots.

"You're that close now. Here we are. There's a pair for the lady and a pair for her brother. You'll not be minding that they're different colors, so long as they're for different feet. Just pull them over your nice shoes."

"I'll be right back," Kerry said. "I left our camera in the car."

"I thought there was something odd about them," the landowner said with a wink to Frank. "Two Yanks, I thought, and no camera."

He led Danny to a gate in a post-and-wire fence. "Here's the path, as plain as plain. Up over the hill and then you'll see the village in the valley beyond."

The hill they gazed up was, to Danny's New Jersey eye, a small mountain. It was treeless, like the true mountains she could see on every horizon, but alive with grass and thorny bushes where the distant ones were dead and stony. Of the "sheep and more sheep" they'd been promised back at the cultural center, there was no sign.

She'd have asked after them to pass the time, but Kerry

rejoined them then. He was zipping himself up in the plastic jacket she'd bought him at the cultural center, which was even more red than their mud-spattered car.

"We'll not lose you at least," Reagan said approvingly. "And while we're on the subject, promise me you'll get back here while it's still light. You can bump your head on the dark in these parts; it's that hard. Whatever you do, don't get benighted."

"Now you tell us," Kerry said.

CHAPTER FORTY-FIVE

"Following your story's dramatic climax,
there should be an emotional one."
—Camelot Guide to Romance Writing

They started off, Danny in front, Kerry in the middle, and Frank behind. The path was kind in its layout, rising in gentle switchbacks, but not in its footing. The eternal rain had exposed stone after stone, some loose and unstable underfoot and others as fixed and abrupt as headstones. To protect their ankles they had to climb with their eyes down, so that Danny missed much of the scrubby plant life around her and the slow clearing of the sky, which Conneely had predicted.

From time to time the path was cut across diagonally by freely flowing, tumbling streams. The Americans sloshed through these fearlessly in their rubber boots, until Kerry noticed that one of his had a hole in it. After that he tried to imitate Frank's practice of jumping across or balancing on stones.

Following a particularly unsuccessful attempt, Kerry forced a halt while he emptied a flooded boot. "Protect us from the damp, Ned said. Some damp. You could drown in it."

"He has a talent for understatement, our Mr. Reagan," Frank agreed. "But we're almost to the top."

Danny reached it first and found a broad expanse of naked stone dotted with little pools of water, each one reflecting a sky now perfectly blue. Beyond was the valley, a very sloping valley, running down from the Maamturk foothills on Danny's left to the barely visible highway far off to her right.

In the middle of this undulating plain was the promised grove of trees and before them the rough brown outlines of huts and houses, looking at this distance like a construction of toy blocks, left unfinished.

"Letterfenny," Kerry said. He had come up beside his sister unnoticed. "Damn. I never thought we'd actually see it."

"We haven't seen it yet," Danny said. "Not like we will."

"I'm content with this. We found it."

They had been standing shoulder to shoulder, with Frank some way off, pretending to ignore them. Danny now followed the Irishman's example, distancing herself from her brother a cautionary step or two.

"No way," she said. "We wouldn't even be on the plane home before you'd be complaining about not actually setting foot in the place. I'm not going to let this turn into something you'll always regret."

"It'd be low on my list, Sis."

Earlier in the week, that wistful statement of the case would have swayed Danny. But not on this day. Not on this bald hilltop in wild Connemara. Not after all they'd been through. She listened to her brother's regular breathing and decided she was being played again.

Still, she was moved enough to give Kerry a chance to save himself the hike by making a clean breast of things at last. "After all," she said, "this is why we came to Ireland. Isn't it?"

That terminal question proved to be too much, an extra jiggling of the line that scared the fish away. As far away, at least, as a squarish stone outcropping, where the fish sat himself down.

Danny could see that Kerry's face was drawn, the lines radiating from the eyes and the parallel ones on his forehead suddenly deep cut. So deep that Danny was granted a passing vision of how Kerry might look at sixty.

"It's not that much farther," she said.

"I'm not going on, Danny. If Letterfenny was no farther away than I can piss—pardon my Gaelic—I wouldn't finish this hike. I'm not going to set foot in that place."

"Why not?"

"Because it's a boneyard, and I'll be in one soon enough and long enough. Tombs and graveyards and ruins, they're everywhere you look in this country. If I'd remembered that, I would have thought twice before I dragged you back over here."

"Why did you drag me here?" Danny asked, not ungently.

"So Bridey Finnerman could rest in peace," Kerry said, and smiled at that. "Or maybe so I would."

"You're not dying," Danny said. "You've got the good kind of leukemia. The slow kind."

"Chronic lymphocytic leukemia," Kerry said, nodding. "Strange how you can get so attached to something so lousy. And sad."

"Why sad?"

"Because I may have gotten one of those words wrong. The doctor may actually have said acute lymphocytic leukemia, the kind that kills you fast."

Danny felt Frank's hand on her shoulder. "And your doctor let you come over here?" she asked.

"No. He started setting up treatments right away. When I called him from Limerick about my prescriptions, he was mildly upset. But only mildly. That told me reams about my prognosis.

"Sorry to spring it on you like this, but I don't expect you're that surprised. You figured out I've been drinking water most of the week."

"I didn't. Max told me."

"Max. Sorry about that. I'm not exactly sure why I asked

him along. I'm worried about you being alone, of course. I mean, I was worried about that. But I think I was really hoping that Max would shake things up. Turns out we didn't need him for that either."

"Why did you need anyone to shake things up?"

"For immortality through art. Although I have to say, this ghost story of yours has me rethinking the whole immortality issue."

He studied his sister's face. "Left you behind again, have I? Have you forgotten John Wayne's match?" Kerry mimicked the striking of a match on a roof beam and the lighting of a cigarette.

Danny remembered, from the swirl of bits and pieces of the week, the match that John Wayne had struck against his cottage rafter, the movie match Kerry had envied for its infinite number of lives. And she remembered something else: Conneely's parting injunction to tell their mutual story. And the old man's judgment that it was important for Danny to tell it, that telling the story was the point of it all. At the time Conneely said it, Danny had thought only of Bridey and Seamus Finnerman and the lost Michael Robart. But now . . .

Kerry saw the dawning in her eyes and nodded.

"What now?" asked Frank, for whom no sun had risen.

"I don't have time enough left to write a novel of my own," Kerry explained. "I cried in my beer the night that sunk in. Then it occurred to me that I could still inspire one, if I could just get Danny here off somewhere for a week or so and tangle her in every crazy thing that came our way."

"You didn't think she had enough material on you already?"

"Who wants to be in a book like that? *I Remember Kerry*. That'd rush off the shelves. The life and times of a barely average guy. I wanted it to be an adventure story. Something picaresque, or at least picturesque. 'Better to pass boldly into that other world, in the full glory of some passion, than fade and wither dismally with age.' That's from something by James Joyce, give or take a preposition. 'The Dead.' "

"Our friend Conneely's favorite," Danny said.

"Well, it's a great story and great advice. You two can supply the passion. Now, get on to Letterfenny. We have to have an ending."

" 'It's only in your minor stories that everything is worked out,' " Danny quoted. "If you want art, we should stop right here."

"Well, let's aim for art and hope we hit something. You can always put Letterfenny in an epilogue. Have a grand walk."

Epilogue:
Letterfenny

Danny's eyes were streaming before she'd walked a dozen steps. Frank's too, she noted. The wind, she told herself, and that was surely part of it, for the breeze had freshened while they'd loitered in the sun. The downhill trek was very like the up, but drier. And faster in spite of the wind, with Frank taking the lead.

He continued to set the pace on the valley floor. There Letterfenny would disappear, Brigadoon-like, as they slogged across boggy low points. Then the grove of trees would reemerge as they climbed to firm sunlit ground, and always a little nearer.

The rise and fall of the valley floor at last gave way to a modest climb. Now the ruins were steadily in view. Stone walls that had seemed a homogenous tan from a distance became a motley of browns and grays and even greens. Proximity gave this variety but took away the illusion that walls were regular if incomplete. Danny now saw that every one was topped by a ragged line, as though their upper parts had been torn from them by an angry hand. She hadn't noticed a boundary wall around the ruined village from their vantage point on Reagan's hill, but they came upon a trace of one now, almost hidden in the grass. Frank didn't trouble himself with steering them toward a gap in this survivor, as it was no more than three stones high anywhere within sight.

Just shy of the perimeter, he pulled them up. "Will she be in there waiting for us, do you think? Your Bridey?"

They'd done very little talking the previous evening after the police and Kerry and Conneely had left them alone. Almost no talking, though they'd clung together through the night. And this was the subject they hadn't been talking about, Danny now realized. Bridey.

"She might be there. She seems to like ruins."

"Do you think Finnerman could see her in your room last night?"

"I don't know."

"I couldn't," Frank said. "Could you?"

"No." Danny felt an odd regret at the idea that Bridey might have been there but invisible to her, that she might never see her again.

Frank asked, "Do you ever see ghosts in America?"

"Never."

"Well then. That settles the question of residency as far as I'm concerned." He took in a good breath. "Let's do the thing."

They stepped hand-in-hand across the barrier and stood in Letterfenny at last.

Here it comes, Danny thought.

She'd been imagining the moment all week, and every imagining had provoked the choking sense of isolation she'd felt on the airliner coming over, felt whenever she'd thought of Kerry gone.

She braced herself for it now. And it didn't come. Her eyes were dry—the wind was blocked by the ancestral grove, planted for that purpose—and she felt at peace. More than that, she felt at home, as though, when they'd stepped across the tiny wall, they'd landed magically in her own New Jersey.

Together they explored the ruins: first the little collection of cottages built wall against wall for mutual support at the village's lower end, then two fine buildings side by side above that, and finally a lone house above the rest with one intact wall that ended in the outline of a steep gable.

Though never far from her—often holding her hand—Frank was very quiet. In the Hollywood version of the moment, he would have had some line to say to sum up the play they'd enacted together. But he didn't sum things up. Instead, he kissed her, unmindful of ghosts.

Danny had no way of knowing which of the houses had been her grandfather's birthplace, so she chose one, the one she would have picked for herself, the one highest on the hill and the most set apart. She led Frank back up to it and, seized by the sudden desire to share the moment with Kerry, she stepped up onto a wall that had all but fallen in at one corner. She used this low point as the first step in a staircase—an irregular and even shifting one. With Frank first steadying her and then cajoling her, she ascended, arms outstretched. When she reached the intact corner where her stairway met the end wall, she braced herself against the skyward-pointing gable and looked out across the valley. She saw the stone-capped hill and, near its flat peak, a figure in red.

Perched there teetering, Danny raised one arm above her head and received an answering wave.

Then her eye was caught by a movement behind her brother. She saw a second figure at the very peak of the hill, a mere blur of brown, waving a bright bit of blue.

ABOUT THE AUTHOR

Terence Faherty is the author of thirteen novels, three novellas, and two short story collections, including six books in the Shamus-winning Scott Elliott private-eye series set in the golden age of Hollywood and nine books in the Macavity-winning and Edgar-nominated Owen Keane series, which follows the adventures of a failed seminarian turned amateur sleuth. Faherty's short stories have appeared in *Ellery Queen Mystery Magazine, Alfred Hitchcock Mystery Magazine,* and *The Strand Magazine,* and in anthologies published in the United States and the United Kingdom. His novels have been reissued in Germany, Italy, and Japan. Faherty, a sometime lecturer on the films of Basil Rathbone, lives in Indianapolis, Indiana, with his wife Jan.